Wave I

CW01465145

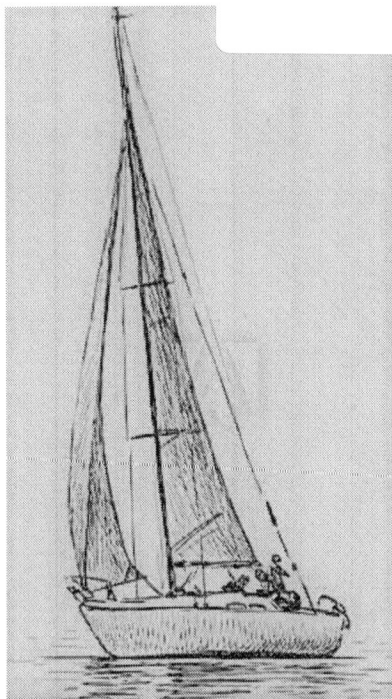

By

Tom Balch

Copyright

This book is a work of fiction. Names, characters, businesses, organisations. and events are either the product of the author´s imagination or are used fictitiously. Any resemblance to actual persons, living or dead, events or locales is entirely coincidental.

Copyright © 2021 Tom Balch, Villanueve De Algaidas, Malaga. All Rights Reserved. No part of this book may be reproduced or transmitted in any form or by any means without written permission from the author.

Dedicated to:

JM and PM

This book is also dedicated to all those people whose dreams never come to fruition. May their luck change for the better.

The Chapters

Wave Dancer

Chapter One

'The Storm, January 2011'

It was a bitter cold January evening; The fire was doing its best to warm the inside of the little brick boathouse built into the rock but failing miserably.
Outside the wind was up and howling at the door and shutters, threatening to burst in and wreak all kinds of havoc.
Waves were crashing onto the rocks and spraying up into the air to a height of twenty feet, and anything not tied down would be washed away. The thunderous rumble of the pebbles being stirred up by an angry sea was deafening.
The flagstone floor was cold and stealing the heat from the inside of Dan Bridge´s coastal 'Hermit' hideaway.
He sat in his solid oak Captain's chair as close to the fire as he could get, his hands wrapped around the mug of steaming strong coffee he had just made and he thought to himself 'Well, no one ever told me that life would be easy'.

As he sipped his coffee, he was looking around to see if there was anything he could lay on the floor as some sort of insulation. Apart from his waterproof clothing and the old nets there really wasn't anything that would do.

Dan was running low on logs for the fire, but in the log store which was twenty yards from the old boathouse there were logs in abundance, and some coal left over from last year 'about three buckets full' but making that trip in this weather would be treacherous and nothing short of foolhardy.

He had no choice but to stay boarded up inside and wait out the storm. The pot of stew he made a few days ago had lasted well and food wise he had plenty to see him through, certainly till the storm is over.

The boathouse was divided into two areas, the slip way end 'where his clinker-built rowing boat was housed' and a living area. A small door had been built into the partition.

At the far end double doors opened up onto the slip way to allow for the launching of his boat.

At the top end nearest the living area there was a washroom which housed a shower cubicle and was basin.

In the living area there was a cast iron log or coal burner, a wardrobe, chest of four drawers, a small table, a gas stove, his oak Captains chair, a bunk bed, and a fridge freezer.

Outside the rain was belting down on the tin roof and coupled with the noise of the storm it would be enough to send any normal person running for the comfort of the town. Dan though, only knew this way of life and to him it was no hardship.

He poured himself another coffee from the pot on the stove and made himself a sandwich of cheese and Branston pickle, 'his favourite'.

As he sat back down there was an almighty crashing noise that came from the slipway end of the boathouse. He put down his coffee and went through the partition door to see what had happened. The double doors at the far end had blown open and were banging in the gale force wind.

He went back into the living area and put on his waterproofs and boots; No way was he going to risk getting soaked. The bottom bolt that secures the doors to the floor had been ripped off so the only way to secure them was to tie them together and hammer wedges under both the doors to stop them being blow inwards.

Once the wedges had been hammered in place, he propped the two doors with beams from the top of the doors to the floor, this made the makeshift repair stable and should certainly hold till the storm dies out.

When he had finished securing the doors, he decided to check outside to see if it was possible to get to the log store safely.

The waves were blasting the rocks and it was impossible for him to make it along the narrow ledge to the store.

He went back inside and finished his sandwich and coffee then threw the last of the logs into the burner. Making sure everything was safe inside he got into his bunk, wrapped up warm and fell into a sound and much needed sleep.

The following morning he awoke to silence from outside, silence that is, compared to the noise of the storm. He opened the shutters and looked out of the window; it was like a normal day. The storm was over, and all was calm outside.

His first chore was to restock with logs and bring in the remaining coal from the log store, then relight the fire as it had gone out during the night.

As he made his way to the store, he noticed that there was a lot of debris washed up onto the beach of the small cove. It looked 'from where he was' that it was pieces from a yacht. He went down to the shoreline which looked like the aftermath of World War Three. All sorts had been washed ashore in the storm. There were lots of pieces

from a small boat, blue and white in colour. As he was pulling the largest piece
from the water's edge, he noticed a body on the pebbles about ten feet or so from the boathouse.

The body was that of a male and dressed in sailing gear. He confirmed that the man was dead before dragging his body up the slipway and into the boathouse. He then radioed the coastguard to inform them of the body and the boat pieces he had found.

Bernard Wilson the coastguard 'Bernie' to his friends told Dan that he would inform the Police and that someone would be with him soon. He also told Dan that there was an SOS sent out by a yacht called 'Wave Dancer' at four in the morning and that there were two people on board.

Lifeboats were sent out to search but nothing had been found, he told Dan that he would redirect the search crews to the new search area in hope of finding the second person.

Dan collected the last of the coal and made a few trips stocking up with logs, he got the fire going and made himself a bowl of porridge for breakfast while he waited for the Police to arrive.

A few hours later the police arrived with the medical examiner and after examining the body it was taken away. The police carried out a search of the beach and the cove but there was no sign of the other person. The police told Dan that they would continue their search along the coast and if he was to find anything, he was to inform them.

Dan spent the afternoon repairing the slipway doors and cleaning up after the storm. As he worked, he couldn´t help but think about how the 'Wave Dancer' came to be broken up and washed ashore in the cove.

'She must have struck the rocks east of here just off Prawle Point' he thought, broke up and parts of her carried in on the incoming tide. With the force and direction of the storm she may have washed up as far down the coast as Gara rock to the west.

He decided that in the morning he would take his rowboat 'with the outboard motor attached' to Prawle Point and follow the coastline all the way down to Gara Rock to see if he could find anymore parts of the wreckage or in fact the boat itself.

That evening Dan sat outside with a cup of coffee, the tide was on its way out and for January it was quite a lovely evening. The wind had dropped, and the sea had calmed, it was totally different from the past few days.

The coastguard vessels had been searching up and down the coastline but came up empty handed, Dan had collected a pile of broken pieces from

'Wave Dancer' and stacked them all by the log store ready for the police to take them away or examine them.

As he sat looking out to sea enjoying the winter sunset, he noticed something orange coloured bobbing in the water about a hundred meters from the shore, he went inside and got his binoculars and on looking again he saw it was a person in a life jacket.

Quickly he ran to the slip way and launched his boat, the outboard motor started on the first pull of the cord and he turned and headed to the body.

As he got nearer, he could see that it was a woman and she seemed to be alive. He pulled the boat alongside her and pulled her onboard.   She was breathing but not moving, he sped back to shore and carried her into the boat house. She started to come around after Dan had placed her by the fire. He made her a mug of strong sweet tea and gave her some dry clothes to change into.

She told Dan that the yacht she was on broke up in the storm during the night and that her friend had been washed overboard. She was totally exhausted and kept falling asleep.

Dan contacted the police and informed them about the woman he had rescued, and they said that someone would be with him soon. They also said that they would arrange for an ambulance.

The woman told Dan that her name was Jill Marshall and that she and her friend had sailed out of Alderney in the Channel Islands heading for Langston Harbour when the storm kicked in.

She said that they were sailing with just a reefed mainsail but there was no way that they could maintain a steady course. Geoff Taylor her friend and the skipper of the yacht was lost overboard when they struck rocks.

"I have no idea where we were or what heading we were on; it was really frightening. The wind was strong, and the waves were smashing into us. It was dark and…" She started sobbing as she relived the experience.

"Are you warming up a bit now" asked Dan. "Yes, thank you" she replied still trembling with the cold. "I'm starting to feel my feet and hands again.

"You're an incredibly lucky lady" said Dan, "I was getting ready to go inside and lock up for the night when I spotted your life jacket, another few minutes and it would have been too late". Looking at the clock on the wall Dan said, "The ambulance should be here soon, they'll take care of you and check you over".

Dan got another blanket and put it around her shoulders. "Here, let me get you some more tea" he said taking her cup. Dan thought it was best not to mention the death of her friend Geoff and that it may be better coming from the police when they get here.

The police and ambulance arrived together, and the paramedics checked her over before taking her to the hospital. The police took down her name and address and confirmed that the yacht she was on, was in fact 'Wave Dancer'.

After thanking Dan for his actions the police officer said his goodbyes and made his way up the path to his patrol car and then followed the ambulance to the hospital.

When Dan went back inside, he realized that the women's clothes were still draped over the line above the log burner, so he phoned the police station to let them know. The station officer said that he would get someone out there to collect them as soon as he could.

Dan turned the clothes round to help them dry and as he did so a small plastic screw top container fell out of the waterproof jacket pocket onto the floor, he picked it up and noticed that it had cracked on the stone floor and a piece had broken off. He unscrewed the top and inside there was cash, a set of keys and a folded-up piece of paper, he unfolded the paper and written on it was some sort of code or note…

'The Voters are armed with Forks, and the Chair is owned by other gents. BRHC of D, 6R 3U, when removed reveals the final piece'

"No idea what this means" he said to himself as he put the contents back inside the container. After a few moments though Dan decided to make a copy of the code, why he wasn´t sure but it seemed to him that it was the right thing to do.

Dan taped the broken piece of plastic to the container with Sellotape and replaced it in the jacket pocket as he did so there was a knock on the door, he opened the door and there was a young police officer who had come to collect Miss Marshall´s clothes.

"Come in officer, her clothes are not quite dry yet but I´ll bag them up for you, I´ve got some Tesco carrier bags I can put them in".

"That´ll be great, thank you," said the officer.

"How is she by the way" asked Dan. "I´m not sure Sir, but from what people were saying earlier she seems to be okay. I´ll be taking her clothes straight to the hospital from here, if you give me your number I can ring and update you later".

"Thank you, officer, I´d appreciate it if it´s not too much trouble".

"Not at all Sir, after all you are the hero in this,

everyone is talking about it at the station".

I don´t know about 'Hero' it was pure luck that I spotted her and the fact that she was wearing a life jacket is probable why she´s alive today".

"Either way sir, the Inspector at the station says that you should get some kind of award or medal for you actions".

"As long as she is well, that´s all that matters," said Dan.

The young officer took the carrier bags, said goodnight, and assured Dan that he would call later with an update on how she was, he then made his way up the track to his patrol car.

The young officer 'true to his word' called Dan later that evening and informed him that Miss Marshall was indeed well but they will keep her in overnight as a precaution.

The following morning Dan was up early, more debris had washed up on the shore so he spent a few hours clearing it up and putting it with the other pieces he found the day before. "The cove certainly looks better now" he said to himself, "Now, methinks a nice cup of coffee will go down well".

His mind went back to the note he found last night in the plastic container, 'What does it mean' he wondered. He went back into the boathouse made himself a nice strong coffee and sat down studying the copy of the note.

"Well" he said out loud, "No one ever told me that life would be easy, and whatever this note means, it won´t be easy to work it out".

"Hello" said Dan answering the phone. It was Jill Marshall; she had been discharged from hospital and was staying at a B & B in the village. "If it is convenient, I would like to call in and return the clothes you gave me, also to thank you for saving me from what would have been a rather unpleasant watery grave".

Dan told her it would be fine and that he would be in all day.

-:T:-

Chapter Two

'The Letter in the Book'

Jill Marshal arrived at the boathouse at three o'clock in the afternoon.

"Well, you certainly look a lot better than you did the last time I saw you" said Dan as he opened the door. "Please, come in, I have some coffee on the go".

"Yes, I feel a lot better now thank you" she said "The doctors have checked all the vitals and given me a clean bill of health. I am so grateful to you for all you did the other night. It was a good thing that I was wearing a wet suit under my waterproofs. They say the coldness of the water could have killed me".

"The important thing is that you are well and in the land of the living," said Dan.

As they sat sipping their coffee Dan was considering when to bring up the subject of the note, but before he could mention it, Jill started to explain.

"A year ago whilst Geoff was waiting for a train at York railway station, he found a book that someone had left in the waiting room. Between its pages was a letter containing clues that would apparently lead the finder to so called 'Riches' beyond his or her wildest dreams.

The other night we were on our way from Alderney to Langston following the final clue.

Geoff had worked out that the clues were based on the App 'what3words'. Have you heard of it?" she asked Dan.

"Can´t say I have" he replied with a somewhat baffled look on his face.

"Well" said Jill, "It´s an App that can tell a position anywhere in the world using three words. It is based on a three meter square system, each square is given a unique three word code. If you have a mobile or a laptop I can show you".

"I´ve got a laptop but I only use it for my writing, there´s no internet here I´m afraid" said Dan, who´s curiosity was now starting to get the better of him.

"Not to worry" said Jill, and she continued telling her story, "The clue we were following to Langston is the last of the five original clues.

At each of the locations the clues lead us to, there is a small tin that is wrapped in plastic and hidden somewhere in the three square meters, and they are not easy to find. Inside each tin there is a coded message that leads us to the next location.

When we find the last tin it should give us the final destination".

"It all sounds a bit farfetched if you ask me" said Dan, "How do you know that when you get to the final position that you won´t be greeted with a big fat April fool?".

"We don´t" said Jill, "But the thrill and the fun of the chase 'as they say' is certainly well worth our time".

"So, what will you do now, I mean with the death of Geoff and the loss of 'Wave Dancer', will you continue on your own or abandoned the search?" Dan asked, getting really interested now.

"Well, Geoff´s body is being taken to his home in York next week, his mother wants his funeral held there, and after his cremation she will scatter his ashes in the river Ouse at Naburn Marina, that´s where his love of boats and life on the water was born and developed".

"Were you close to Geoff?" asked Dan.

"We were sailing buddies, we weren´t in a relationship, just good friends. We met years ago in Cowes, I was on my father's yacht taking part in the round island race and Geoff was crewing for us, since then we´ve sailed most weekends in and around the Solent.

In Geoff´s study at his home in York he has all of the clues, the letter, the maps…. and yes, I do think that I will continue the search, not so much for the riches it promises but more for Geoff really, he would love for me to see it through and finish what he started".

"So the 'Riches' are not a factor in this then" said Dan smiling.

"No" said Jill "We are both well off and come from very wealthy families, it´s all about living life to the full for us".

"Well, if you do intend to continue and need a good deck hand".

"What! you would join me, is that what you are saying?" asked Jill.

"It is indeed" said Dan. "It all sounds fascinating to me and I would absolutely love to be a part of such an adventure, so, if I´ve passed the audition where do I sign" Dan said laughing.

"Okay, you're on. I shall be back after the funeral in two, maybe three weeks' time and I´ll bring all of the paperwork, clues and stuff with me. We can go through it all and bring you up to speed. Will I be able to moor up my Arvor weekender on your slipway, I think we´ll use motor as opposed to sail next time, do it in style" Jill said laughing.

"That´s fine with me" said Dan, "and yes, the Arvor will be fine moored here there is plenty of depth, even when the tide is out".

Over the next hour they chatted about all manner of things and it seemed to Jill that they would make a great team working together.

Jill told Dan that she lived in Yarmouth on the Isle of Wight and that she had a house with a private dock in High Street backing onto the Solent. The Arvor is moored in Yarmouth harbour as 'Wave Dancer' used to be.

The Arvor is named 'Solent Sam', Sam after her late father. He spent most of his life sailing in the Solent and used to run RYA (*Royal Yachting Association*) courses, Competent Crew   Deck hand, Day skipper and Coastal Skipper.

Jill helped out with the courses whenever she was free to do so, she just loved being around boats and the harbour. "It's in the blood" she'd say.

When Jill had left, Dan started to apply his mind and plan what he would need to pack or get ready for the trip. Over the next few days he ordered in and stocked up on logs for the log burner and spent a few days clearing up the cove.

He wanted everything to be in good order if he was to be going away for a while.

Dan could not believe that Jill was coming in an 'Arvor Weekender' to him it was the perfect little craft he'd always dreamed of owning. Made in Australia, nine meters in length, two berth, and a small galley, just right for coast hopping, fishing, and sleeping in. It would suit his lifestyle perfectly he thought. "If we do find the reward that the letter promises then it will certainly be on my shopping list", he told himself. "Might even call it Solent Dan" he said laughing out loud, "Solent Sam´s younger brother". His excitement was now really starting to mount.

Whilst Jill was away Dan had upgraded his land line with fibre optic broadband, purchased himself a Samsung Smart Phone and had the time of his life learning all about his new digital world. He was absolutely amazed with the App 'what3words' and thought it was quite brilliant that someone would use it for a treasure hunt.

-:T:-

Chapter Three

'Goodbye Geoff'

Jill had driven up to York and booked into the York Hilton on Tower Street, she had stayed there many times before and found it to be perfectly situated for shopping, especially with Fenwick's just around the corner. She planned to visit Geoff's mother Cynthia the following afternoon at her beautiful Grade II listed home in Precentor's Court just opposite York Minster.

Geoff's home was just off Tadcaster Road near 'The Tyburn' overlooking the Knavesmire and the wonderful York racecourse. She arrived there at three o'clock and let herself in with the set of keys that Geoff had given her. The house was used as their base for the 'letter in the book' adventure as he referred to it.

In his study Jill collected up the original letter, the book, and the clues still in their tins. She also took the working notes and journal Geoff and she had worked on over the last twelve months.

There was also the photographs of each of the locations. She put everything into a large cardboard box locked up and went to her car.

When she had put the box into the boot, she

looked back at the house one last time saying out loud to herself "We won't let you down, Geoff , goodbye my friend and rest peacefully".

She then made her way back to the Hotel, parked in the underground car park and went up to her room.

Because of the long drive up to York and the events of the past few days she was now feeling exhausted. She set the alarm on her mobile for seven that evening. "A few hours' sleep will do me a world of good" she thought as she undressed and climbed into a really comfortable and welcoming bed. It didn't take long for her to fall into a deep and restful sleep.

Jill woke to the melody of Frere Jacques, the alarm tune on her mobile. She took the phone from the bedside table and turned off the alarm. She sat up immediately because she was never one to turn over and go back to sleep.

After a nice hot shower she dressed and went down to the reception desk, handed in her room key, turned right out of the hotel and then right again. She walked along to 'The Go Down' restaurant opposite Lower Friergate where she had booked a table for dinner. She and Geoff always ate there whenever she was in York. She ordered a glass of Rioja and the Duck in plum sauce, her favorite meal at the Go Down.

After she had eaten and settled the bill she decided to walk around to the hotel and have a quiet night, maybe she would read a little before going to bed she thought. She collected the book that the letter was found in from her room and made her way to the hotels lounge, settling in one of the lavish armchairs she ordered a Gin and Tonic and began to read. After a while she glanced up at the clock and was surprised to see that she had been reading for quite some time, it was almost half past one. She was so engrossed in the story that she had lost all track of time.

The following morning after a good night's sleep and a large 'Belly Busting' full English breakfast as Geoff would call it, she made her way up to Coppergate to start a few hours of shopping. "It's a hard life" she thought, "But hey, someone has to do it".

Having spent her time in Fenwick's and Marks and Spencer's, laden with carrier bags she headed back to the hotel for a light lunch and rest before making her way to Cynthia's for tea.

Jill received a message while she was having lunch in the hotel restaurant from Cynthia letting her know that she had booked a table at Betty's Tea rooms for three o'clock and to join her there. Jill was thrilled because she always believed that if you are going to have afternoon tea then the best place in the whole world has to be Betty's. Whether in Harrogate, York or Ilkley mattered not, it was always a wonderful experience and something she would highly recommend to anyone. At this moment in time she was really pleased that she had only had a light lunch, she could now have her favourite, a Betty's Yorkshire Fat Rascal Scone, a pot of Orange Pekoe Tea, and of cause the company of Cynthia, whom she absolutely adored.

Jill had known Cynthia for the best part of twenty years. She was in her late sixties, was of medium height, slim, and had an air of nobility about her. Her grey, almost white hair was worn in a bun and she always looked immaculate.

She was very down to earth, soft spoken and the most caring person you could ever wish to meet.

When Jill spoke to her on the phone, she could tell that Cynthia was dying inside. The loss of Geoff had hit her hard, he was her only child and she raised him alone after her husband 'Geoff's father' died when he was only four years old. He died in a violent storm attempting to climb Everest, he and his friend were never found and their bodies are still on the mountain to this day.

Cynthia told Jill during their conversation the other day that she always knew that Geoff would die carrying out some adventure or other. Not only was he the spitting image of his father his character was identical too. "On this earth to live life to the full" she said, "The pair of them cut from the same cloth".

Jill left the hotel at two fifteen turned left and then left again into Castlegate, she walked slowly taking in the atmosphere of the old buildings and churches, she loved walking around York, Geoff always told her that York city was all history, pubs, and churches. After Castlegate she went into Spurriergate leading into Coney street. "How it has all changed" she thought, "Most of the streets are pedestrianised now, but it actually makes it more enjoyable".

At the end of Coney street she went right into Stonegate, Betty´s was on the far right-hand corner and as always people were queuing for the next available table.

Jill went to the counter and told the lady she was meeting Mrs. Taylor and that they had a table booked.

"One moment please" said the lady, she went over to the side and checked the book, came back and said "Yes, Mrs. Taylor is upstairs, please follow me, I´ll take you up".

Jill followed her; Cynthia was at a table set for two at the far end of the room by the window. Her face lit up when she saw Jill and she stood up waiting to hug her when she got to the table.

"How are you, Cynthia?" Jill asked as they hugged.

"Bearing up, Jill, but it´s not easy, is it?" They took their seats and gave their order to the waitress.

Whilst they waited for their tea to arrive Cynthia said "Geoff´s funeral will be held at the York crematorium which is on Bishopthorpe Road next Wednesday morning at eleven o'clock. I would like it if you travelled with me from home in the lead car, I know Geoff would have wanted you to".

" I would like that, Cynthia, thank you".

"Pekoe tea and Fat rascal´s" said the waitress as she placed the order onto the table.

"Thank you" said Cynthia, "Could I please have a small glass of water? I need to take a tablet". "Certainly" said the waitress, "I´ll be back with it shortly" she then went off to get it.

"I love it here" said Jill as she started to pour the tea. "Milk?" she asked.

"No thank you, I prefer it black," said Cynthia. Jill explained that she was going to carry on with the search that she and Geoff had started out on, and that the man who recovered Geoff´s body and rescued her will be helping her.

"I was really hoping that you would see it through" said Cynthia, "I honestly believe that Geoff would have wanted that too".

"That's a relief" said Jill, "I wasn't sure if you would have wanted me to".

"Oh! you do know that Geoff has left you the house and the contents don't you?" Cynthia asked, "After all you are part of the family you know, he often said that you are the sister he never had, he thought the world of you.

The waitress arrived with a glass of water and placed it on the table asking if everything was okay.

"Yes, thank you. Everything is simply perfect" Jill replied, and the waitress told them to call her if there was anything else, they needed.

"I really don't know what to say about the house" said Jill, "It's all come as a big surprise, I'm still trying to process Geoff's death. Everything has happened so quickly. One minute we're sailing out of Alderney on a sunny morning excited about finding the last clue and then the storm hit us...". Cynthia reached across and placed her hand on Jills. "You mustn't torture yourself, Jill" she said in her soft voice, "All we can do is accept what life throws at us, handle it and wait for the next onslaught and between the problems we must treasure and savor the good times".

"As you said a moment ago, Cynthia, it´s not easy, is it?".

"It certainly isn´t" said Cynthia, "Now you must promise me that after the funeral and your adventure you will stay in touch and visit me from time to time".

"Of cause I will" answered Jill, "After all I am part of the family".

The following Wednesday morning Jill arrived at Cynthia´s house at ten forty-five. She arrived early so she could spend some time alone with her before the hearse arrives.

It was a bright morning, not a cloud in the sky, but there was a slight chill in the air.

"I´ve requested that they play Vivaldi´s 'Spring' as his coffin is carried into the chapel, it was one of Geoff´s favourite pieces", said Cynthia, "I´m not sure how many people will be attending but I know that most of his friends from the sailing club will be coming, and after the service we will be having lunch in his honour at the Waterfront café at Naburn Marina yacht club.

It´s going to be a long day, and one with very mixed emotions.

Ready? the hearse has just arrived", said Cynthia.

Those words hit hard, and Jill found herself shedding tears as she looked out of the window and saw the hearse, the coffin, and Geoff´s name spelt out in yellow flowers in the side window.

Black coated chauffeurs stood solemnly by the sides of their limousines, quietly waiting to open doors for the mourners.

The drive down to the crematorium seemed to take forever, and small talk was hard to come by. As they pulled into the driveway of the crematorium Jill reached over and gently squeezed Cynthia´s hand asking, "Are you okay?"

"I´ll be fine dear" she said, "And how about you?" They both smiled a warm smile, exited the car, and made their way into the chapel.

There was about sixty or so people inside, both familiar and unknown faces that were all showing their own sadness. The service was soon over and as the coffin went through the curtains 'O Mio Babbino Caro' sang by Sarah Brightman filled the room. It was a wonderful way to say goodbye to a loved one and a very dear friend.

The Waterfront café at the marina was filled with Geoff´s friends, and the shared memories and stories of his life being exchanged by everyone made an incredibly sad day special.

Cynthia, on the way home came out with that old cliché "I think we done him proud", and Jill replied "Knowing Geoff, he would have loved it Cynthia. Vivaldi and Sarah Brightman, he'd have been in his element. They both laughed, for they knew him well.

-:T:-

Chapter Four

'Solent Sam and Updating Dan'

The day after the funeral Jill loaded up her Land
Rover Evoque, made her way out of York
through Fulford to the A64 and started the long
drive home. As she turned off the A64 onto the
A1, she said out loud as she always did at that
point, "Here we go again, it´s all downhill from
here".

She loved driving, and the long journeys were
not a problem for her.

Her plan was to get down to Southampton and
stay overnight with her friend Paula whom she´d
known from their BT Global Challenge Round
the World sailing days. They were both on the
same leg, Cape Town to Southampton with a
welcomed stop off at La Rochelle for a few
days.

The following morning she would make her
way to Lymington, get the ferry to Yarmouth
and be home by tea time.

On the ferry Jill made her way up on deck with
her coffee. With the wind in her hair and the
smell of the sea it always felt better than being
below decks, and she knew that home was not

too far away now.

When she arrives home she will spend a few days doing absolutely nothing. She will rest up and re-coop, a promise she made to herself after Geoff's funeral, and a promise that she intends to keep.

The weekend was spent finishing the book she started reading at the hotel, 'A Doorway in Blake Street' written by some author she had never even heard of, but because she enjoyed reading it so much she will certainly be buying his next book.

On the Monday morning, fully rested and feeling better than she had done for weeks, she made a flask of coffee, a few sandwiches and then went down to the harbour. It was now time for the cleaning and prepping of 'Solent Sam' ready for the next stage in the 'Letter in the book' adventure.

Jill spent hours cleaning the Arvor, she filled the fresh water tank, filled up with fuel and got two more gas bottles. Tuesday she will stock up on food and fresh rations and leave for Dan's cove on the Wednesday.

Having checked that everything she and Dan needed was on board, Jill slipped her mooring at five a m and headed off to Dan's cove. She had plotted her course on the chart the day before and planned to arrive before nightfall. The weather was kind. There was hardly a breeze and the winter sun was warm on her face. As she passed the Needles a wave of excitement came over her, she knew from old that this always signalled a new adventure was about to unfold.

She kept the boat running at a steady speed of ten knots and never went above 3000rpm.

At the boathouse Dan was up early and preparing a breakfast of egg on toast, coffee and more toast with Marmalade. He had everything he needed for the adventure packed into his sailing bag and was ready for the off, so it would be a lazy day waiting for Jill to arrive.

Dan had arranged with Bernie Wilson 'the coastguard' to keep an eye on the boathouse while he was away. Bernie lived in the village a few miles inland and he spent a lot of time with Dan out fishing in the row boat. They had been friends for many years and Dan knew that all would be fine in his more than capable hands.

Jill had phoned Dan and let him know that her planned ETA would be around nine o'clock in the evening and Dan promised her that he would have a nice meal waiting.

Jill actually arrived at seven and after she moored up alongside the slipway's jetty both she and Dan sat down to his 'nice' meal of Paella washed down with a few bottles of San Miguel beer.

"This is really good" said Jill pointing to the Paella with her fork, "How did you learn to cook like this?" she asked.

"I've cooked for myself for years" he told her. "Well you are now the new chef on Solent Sam" said Jill laughing. She raised her bottle and they clinked bottles toasting their future adventure.

They decided that the following day would be spent going over the clues and planning their next move.

Dan was up early preparing breakfast for them both. Jill had slept in the Arvor and woke refreshed.

"Something smells worth getting up for" said Jill as she entered the boathouse, "There is nothing in the world that smells better than bacon frying"

"Ha-ha! said Dan, "You can say that again. How d'you like your eggs?" he asked.

"As they come" said Jill "Not fussy at all". After their breakfast they sat in the cabin of the Arvor with mugs of coffee and Jill started the catch up by first showing Dan the letter that was found in the book.

"As you can see, Dan" she said, "It was not

going to be easy at all". Dan read the letter…

*****

'To the finder of this letter'

The following are clues that when solved will lead you to 'Riches' beyond your wildest dreams. You have two years to solve the clues and find your reward. After the two year period the clues will become invalid and the reward removed from its location. The two year period will start on January 1st, 2010 at 1200 hrs. There are five clues and each clue will lead to the next.

'This is Not a hoax'

Good luck, and may your journey be successful.

(ADIBS) 97986639049771 90000

Seven, nineteen, one
One hundred and three, ten, one.
One hundred and ninety four, six, eight.

Clue One

Providing those who have landed by the rivers bank with answers. Where S meets W...

***

"Wow" Said Dan, "How the hell did Geoff get to the 'what3words' App from just looking at this"

"It wasn´t immediate at all" said Jill, "In fact it was a few months before things started to click into place. Geoff must have read the letter a thousand times, and one night he was reading it out loud to me and as he read nine, zero, zero, zero, zero I shouted "Stop" pointed to the book that was face down on the table "It´s the bar code of the book" I said. "Look".

Geoff read out the other numbers and they all matched. "Look" he said "ADIBS, A Doorway in Blake Street, Ha-ha! It´s been in front of us all this time. So, the Seven, Nineteen, one, is a code using this book". "I remember seeing a film once where a 'book code' was used.

The first number was the page, the second was the line down and the third was the word in that line. The code however was useless without the correct book. Spy film I think it was, could have been Sherlock Holmes now I come to think of it." I Said.

"Sherlock, it was" said Geoff "London A to Z if memory serves".

Geoff gave me the book and said "Right, let's see if I´m correct. Page seven".

"I opened the book to that page and then he said. "Line nineteen".

"I counted down to that line and Dan said"
"First word of that line"
"WHAT" the first word is WHAT" I said getting really excited. Geoff wrote it down and then read out the second row of numbers. I found the page, counted down and along. "THREE" I said.

Geoff wrote that down as well. We done the same with the third line of numbers. "WORDS" I said.

"Well we now have 'what three words'. What the hell does that mean?" asked Geoff.

"Google it" I said. He did so and we found out that it´s an App that you can get from Google play. We both downloaded and installed the app on our mobiles. Geoff read out the clue and said

"I reckon the first part of the clue has the three words we need to find the location and the second part will tell us where to look. What we have to do is go through every permutation of the words to get the ones we want".

"Hang on, look" I said, "The words 'Providing, Landed and Rivers are in a different type of font to the rest, try them".

"Geoff type those words in and we came up with somewhere in Cumbria. He tapped the words and it was a place called 'Watendlath' Tarn in the Lake District. He changed the view to satellite from the map view and we could see that the square was where the wall and the fence meet the water.
We then turned on Google Earth, went to the same place and 'EURIKA' we confirmed our first location"

"If you hadn't noticed the numbers on the bar code or the different font" said Dan "You would never have got it"

"The other thing of cause" said Jill "Is that if Geoff had only kept the letter and not the book it would have been impossible to solve".

Dan picked up the book and said "So this was the key to it all"
"It's a great story, Dan, you should give it a read" said Jill.

We decided that we would drive up to the Lake District the following week. I found out that there was a walkers route to the Watendlath Tarn from the village of Rosthaite and it takes only a few hours to get there.

Geoff had been on line and found the 'Hazel Bank Country Hotel' in Rosthaite and booked two rooms for two nights.

"Going to need your walking boots and back pack" Geoff said as he looked up from his laptop. "We might as well enjoy the lakes while we are there".

"I have never been to the Lake District" I told him. "I´m quite looking forward to the trip".

"You will fall in love with the place the moment you see your first mountain and lake" he said. "It truly is a beautiful place. Tell you what, when we´ve found the clue we can book into a hotel in Ambleside for a few days, might even drag you up Scarfel Pike".

"And what is Scarfel Pike when it´s at home" asked Jill.

"The highest mountain in England" said Geoff, "Oh well, in for a penny" said Jill shrugging her shoulders.

-:T:-

Chapter Five

'Watendlath and Towton'

The following week we left Geoff´s house on the Tuesday morning and drove up to our first stop which was at Scotch Corner on the A1 where we called in for a coffee and Geoff´s favourite a cream filled chocolate éclair, which as it turned out was fast becoming my favourite too.

Then it was the A66 to Keswick and down through to Rosthaite.

We arrived at the Hazel Bank Country Hotel at three in the afternoon and it did not disappoint.

Set in the heart of Lakeland this gem was the perfect place to stay and it was easy to see how it was listed as five star.

The rooms were beautifully decorated and the views were stunning. Having settled into our rooms we met up in the lounge where a log fire added to the ambiance. We booked a table for dinner in the hotel´s restaurant for eight that evening and then spent a few hours sat by the fire in luxurious armchairs enjoying a pot of tea, sandwiches and 'what Geoff insisted on having' a slice of fruit cake.

During tea we got talking to one of the waiters, a pleasant lad by the name of Martin, he told us that the route up to Watendlath Tarn was easy to follow and said that it would be raining all day tomorrow "That's normal in the Lakes for this time of year" he said, "The kitchen can make up flasks and pack lunches if you would like".

"That would be great" Geoff told him, and ordered for two.

Ha-ha! Martin was right, the next morning it was absolutely chucking it down as we started out on our trek up to the Tarn.

Wrapped up in our fleeces and waterproofs we followed the river and the signs to Watendlath.

Geoff told me on the drive from York that it mattered not what the weather was doing, it will never take away the beauty of the Lake District.

As we made our way along the narrow tracks that meandered their way through the woods and fields of Borrowdale in the pouring rain it was impossible to disagree with him.

The views were just breath-taking and we would stop every now and again to look back and enjoy the stunning scenery.

When we finally arrived at Watendlath Tarn we followed the track round the left of the tarn which took us over a beautiful stone bridge and into the Hamlet. There was a tea room and a few houses. Looking down to the tarn we could see the stone wall and the fence leading into the water and

Geoff said "We´re here Jill, the three meter square is there look, just at the end of the wall".

Luckily, the rain had eased off and the day was certainly brighter than when we set off earlier. We made our way down to the water's edge and sat on our backpacks by the stone wall.

"Tea and a sandwich before we start searching" said Geoff.

"Yes please" I said, "I´m really not used to this hill walking and my legs are aching a bit"

"Whilst drinking our tea, Geoff went over the notes he made and the clue itself. "Well this is the square, the clue could be where we are sat, in the water or buried somewhere. The clue says, *'Where S meets W'*, I´ve no idea what that means. South meets West, something meets water. Another sandwich?" asked Geoff.

"Yes please, I´m starving, it must be all the fresh air and exercise" I said. "Stones meets water. Ha-ha! How about *stone* 'as in wall' meets *wood* 'as in wood fence".

"D´yer know what, I think you might be on to something, Jill" said Geoff excitedly. He started looking around the wall where it ended and the fence started, after a few moments he said "Look, this stone seems to be different to the others". It´s a different type of stone altogether".

He got hold of the stone and wiggled it, it came out of the wall with ease. He reached into the gap it left and said "There's something here, Jill". He took out what looked to be a tin that was covered in cling film. After he replaced the stone we removed the cling film and it was a green 'Golden Virginia' two once tobacco tin.

Shaking it, Geoff said "There's something inside. Here you open it, Jill" He handed me the tin, we were like kids at Christmas, excited and giggling I opened the tin. Inside there was a sheet of folded paper. I handed it to Geoff, he unfolded it and read…

"Watendlath Tarn, eighty-nine, three, one, ninety-nine, twenty two, five, and in brackets there are a lot of other numbers. Then it says, *Clue Two, The mass bands will be playing for the importers of goods that will help span the gap".*

"Wow" said Dan, "I bet you both felt pleased with yourselves, I know I would have been".

"We did, we were, we gave each other high fives wearing the biggest grins you could ever imagine. We decided not to try decoding it until we got back to the hotel". We packed the flask and the sandwich box away, put on our back packs and headed back to Rosthaite.

Jill handed the note to Dan and gave him time to read it.

***

'Watendlath Tarn'

89, 3, 1, 99, 22, 5

(28, 14, 5, 64, 1, 3, 170, 7, 5, 6, 16, 3, 61, 6, 4, 184, 12, 7, 190,16, 3.)

Clue Two
The mass bands will be playing for the Importers of goods that will help span the gap.

***

"I see that there are more numbers this time and all of the words are in the same type of font" said Dan.

"Yes" said Jill "And that threw us, it meant we had to do a lot more work to solve it, and it was not going to be easy".

"I would have started with the numbers" said

Dan, "If they are used with the same book, that is".

"We did and they were" said Jill, "The numbers were straight forward using the same system as before. We de-coded them that evening at the hotel and they spelt out the following.

'Well done you are one down four to go'

We spent quite a few day's going through every permutation possible and eventually came up with *'mass, bands, importers'* this gave us a position just opposite a pub near the villages of Towton and Saxton called 'The Crooked Billet' on the B1217. Geoff couldn't believe it, he had been to that pub many times and said that they serve excellent food".

"We can get this clue on our way back to York" said Geoff "We'll then have two in the bag".

"Wow! I feel great, what a view, I am so pleased we did this" said Jill taking a panoramic shot on her mobile phone from the stone cairn at the top of 'Scafell Pike', England's highest mountain.

"Told you you'd love it" said Geoff taking a selfie of them both. "Ha-ha! Just like Hillary and Tenzing we are".

"We spent four extra day's at a lovely little B&B in Ambleside. Geoff bought a painting by a Lakeland artist called Charles C. Smith, a scene of 'Watendlath Tarn' done in water colours. The nice thing about it was, it depicts the wall and the fence at the water's edge, exactly where we sat and found the first clue, That's the one hanging in his study" said Jill.

"I absolutely adored Ambleside, it's at the top end of Windermere and certainly a place to visit if you get the chance".

"I will add that to my list" said Dan, "I'll go and make us some more coffee, shan't be long".

Dan went to the boat house and put a fresh jug of coffee on and got out a packet of custard creams. "Not as good as cream eclairs" he said to himself, "But I'm sure they'll do".

"Custard creams" said Dan climbing on to the Arvor, "I've totally run out of chocolate covered cream eclairs".

"They will do just fine" said Jill taking her coffee from the tray,

"Okay, where were we?" asked Dan.

"Well" said Jill "We left the lake District and made our way down to Saxton and 'The Crooked Billet' pub, and guess what, we got there just in time for a toasted cheese and onion sandwich and a beer".

"You get all the best jobs" said Dan laughing.

"I know, but someone has to do it" Jill said putting on a fake look of seriousness.

At that moment they were both startled by the opening bars of 'Rule Britannia' Jill's mobile ring tone.

"Hello" she said answering the call. After a short pause she said "Hi Cynthia, how are you" another pause, "Yes of cause I will, what day are we looking at... Yes that's fine.... I'm at Dan's boathouse now, we are going over things and bringing him up to speed on it all...Oh! I'll ask him"

Jill turned and said to Dan, "Cynthia is scattering Geoff's ashes next Tuesday and if you would like to accompany me you are most welcome".

"Yes, of cause. I would like to be there, I feel as though I know him now" Dan replied.

"Yes we shall both be there, Cynthia. We'll drive up on Monday morning, book into the hotel and then pop round to see you in the evening". After a long pause Jill said, "Okay then Cynthia, take care, bye".

"So, we've got... it's Thursday today we've got three day's to get to Langston, find the clue and then get to Yarmouth. What d'you think Dan?".

"Well, I reckon if we head back to the Solent tomorrow morning we´ll have plenty of time".

"That´s what we do then" said Jill.

"I´d best put some decent clothes in a suitcase tonight to take with me" said Dan, "Anyway, you had a cheese and onion toastie and a beer, what happened next?"

"Well, we went over to the other side of the road. In the three meter square there was a bridge that went over a small ditch or beck. It wasn´t large enough to be a river or a stream but there was water running through it".

Geoff said "That now makes sense of the 'Span the gap' sentence in the second clue. It´s got to be somewhere on, around or under the bridge" he said.

We searched along both sides of the small bridge but found nothing. Geoff said, "Knowing my luck it´ll be under the bloody thing in the mud, bet yer!"

He climbed down and disappeared in the thick undergrowth. Every now and again he would let out a small swearword as he got stung by the nettles. At one point he really let rip as he tripped on rocks and fell into the water.

Under the bridge there was a ledge on both sides where the concrete beams ran supporting
he structure. Geoff ran his hand along both, and

at the far end of the right hand side beam he found a length of cord tide to it. He pulled the cord and there was something attached to it in the gap. He eventually pulled it out. There was about eight feet of cord and on the end was tide another tobacco tin wrapped in clingfilm.

All I heard at this point was a really loud 'Eureka' from an excited, wet and badly stung Geoff ".

"We´ll open it when we get to the house" said Geoff rubbing his arms that were absolutely covered in nettle stings.

"Can you see any 'Dock' leaves down there, Jill? he asked. "They´re supposed to be good for stings. There were none, so we headed back to York stopping on the way at Tadcaster. We called into a local chemist and bought a bottle calamine lotion.

"Ah! That´s better" said Geoff, as he applied more than enough of the pink liquid to his arms.

-:T:-

Chapter Six

'The Crooked Billet & The Kings Arms'

"On our way back to the house we called into the chippy´s on Tadcaster road and got two large Haddock and chips to take home for our tea. It had been a busy few day´s and it was starting to catch up on us, so cooking when we get home was not really an option.

"We should have got mushy peas to go with these," said Geoff. Loading up the plates. Geoff opened a bottle of red and we sat in front of the telly with our lap trays.

We decided that we would leave the opening of the tin until the morning when we feel a bit more refreshed".

"You´ve got me thinking about fish and chips now" said Dan. "I can´t remember when I last had some".

"When we get to York next week we´ll make a point of calling in for some on Tad road. You will love them from there, and make sure you ask for scraps" said Jill.

"What do you mean by scraps?" asked Dan. "It´s all the small bits of batter that brake off as the fish fries. It´s a Yorkshire thing, they taste great. They´ll put a scoop full in with your chips if you ask for them".

"Scraps it is then" said Dan, "Ha-ha! so I´ve now got Ambleside, The Lake District, and Scraps on my bucket list, along with an Arvor Weekender of cause".

"You just wait and see" said Jill, "You´ll love them".

Jill took a sip of her coffee and her third custard cream and passed the clue sheet to Dan, saying

"Now, getting back to the clue". This one told us that things were going to get a lot more difficult, see what you make of it".

***

'The Crooked Billet'

D, C, & T Honderdtwintig Acht, =+, Dort,
F, D, & C Limampung apat na, Een, Dva
Clue Three... This time it is not the words in 'Doorway' it is S, Rettel going in reverse.
35, 1, 20/ 25, 15, 43/ 73, 24, 20/ 168, 7, 17/ 190, 28, 41.
23, 1, 2/ 33, 1, 2/ 44, 10, 15/ 57, 5, 1/ 81, 3, 8/ 125, 5, 14.
181, 10, 34/ 189, 1, 23/. 7, 2, 11/ 25, 10, 8. She sits a fathom deep by the limbs of royalty.

***

"Well" said Dan, "You obviously solved it because you were on your way to the last clue on the night of the storm".

"I won't help you just yet, I'll see if you can work it out on your own first. I'm going to have a walk along the cove, stretch my legs a bit".

"Jill jumped down onto the slipway laughing and saying to Dan, "Good luck, let me know when you've got it".

"Thanks a bunch" came the reply from the Arvor's cabin.

"Jill walked down to the shore and then along to the far end of the cove. She turned and looked back at the boathouse and instantly saw why Dan had chosen this place to live. It was indeed the most beautiful and tranquil spot she had ever seen.

She then spotted all of the pieces from 'Wave Dancer' piled up by the log store and made her way over to them.

A chill came over her as she got closer and a deep sadness filled her heart. Not so much for the loss of 'Wave Dancer' but more for the loss of her dear friend Geoff.

"Easy Peasy" came the loud shout from the Arvor. Dan was stood on the deck waving the piece of paper the clue was written on.

"No way have you got it already" shouted Jill,

"I'll be over in a moment" she said still looking at the broken pieces of 'Wave Dancer'.

She noticed that one of the pieces had a small bit 'about two inches square' sawn out of it. Puzzled by this she said to Dan as he arrived at her side, "Did the police cut a piece from this panel".

"No" said Dan, "It was me. I hope you don't mind but I've had my fret saw and sand paper out working on it and I've made you a small key ring 'keepsake' from the piece I cut out. Dan took it from his pocket and gave it to Jill. It was from one of the blue pieces and was in the shape of a yacht.

Dan had attached a small chain and split ring to it. It was about an inch and a half long and he had etched 'Wave Dancer' along its hull.

"Wow! Dan, it's absolutely beautiful, thank you. It really is thoughtful of you".

"I wasn't sure whether to give it to you or not, I didn't know if it would upset you".

"It's a truly wonderful gesture and a lovely reminder, Dan. I love it…. Now, 'Einstein' how on earth did you solve the clue so quickly?".

Dan huffed on his nails and rubbed them on his chest. "It was quite easy for me really, I've spent some time in the Netherlands before and realised that the first part of the clue is to do with languages. "I used Google Translate and came up with the D, C, & T being Dutch, Chinese and

Turkish, that gave me one hundred and twenty eight in Dutch, 'the page number'. Twenty in Chinese for the 'line number', and four was in Turkish for the word, which was 'WELL'.

The next F. D. & C was Filipino, Dutch and Czech and that lead to the word 'DONE'.

I haven't worked out the numbers yet, but 'S. Rettel' backwards or in reverse as the clue says, spells 'LETTERS'. So it´s not words, it´s letters we need to check for in the book". Dan put on one of those 'Am I brilliant or what' type smiles.

"Well, to be honest with you" said Jill, "It took us month´s for the penny to drop. We even Googled S. Rettel wondering who the hell he could possibly be. You´re right, the numbers were letters and the three words it gave us were, Trade, Thinks and Vent.

When we typed them into the 'what3words' app it was a berth in Weymouth just by the pub 'The Kings Arms'. The last part 'She sits a fathom deep by the limbs of royalty' was quite easy.

"Well, until we got there, that is" said Jill.

"We decided that it would be best to head to my home in Yarmouth, ditch the wheels and sail to Weymouth in 'Wave Dancer', and that is exactly what we did do".

" A few days later we arrived in Weymouth and tied up just in front of The Kings Arms, Ha-ha!

and guess what, there was a chip shop next door, Geoff said it was like heaven on earth.

The clue was tied to one of the mooring piles, six feet below the water line at low tide and he had to use his diving gear. He must have searched every inch of that area in front of the pub over the two day´s we stayed there.

The tin was behind one of the piles hidden from view. I won´t tell you what he said when he eventually found it. But at least there were no nettles down there to sting you, I told him when he surfaced.

We both laughed, and more importantly we were both very pleased knowing that we had bagged another clue".

That evening Dan and Jill walked across the fields to the village. They were going to meet up with Bernie Wilson the coastguard at the Pigs Nose pub for a meal. The other reason was to give him a set of keys to the boathouse.

As they walked along the bridle path they chatted about their plans for the next few days.

It was decided that they would leave the cove early in the morning and head straight for Langston harbour. They will moor up at the Langston sailing club and if all goes well they should be heading to Yarmouth the following evening. That would give them a full day to ready themselves for the drive up to York.

As they entered the bar Bernie waved them over to the table he had reserved and after introductions asked what they wanted to drink.

Jill asked for a white wine and Dan for a pint of bitter. "Be right back" said Bernie, "Make yourselves comfy".

Whilst Bernie was at the bar getting the drinks and menu´s for dinner Jill remarked on how full of character and charm the pub was.

"It´s over three hundred years old" said Dan, "It was an old smugglers haunt in those days. It´s where they used to hide all of the contraband from ships that had come to grief on the rocks.

This entire coastline in days long gone was rife with smuggling and shipwrecks.

"One white wine and a pint of bitter" said Bernie placing their drinks on the table, "And a menu each. You´ll like the food here Jill, I can recommend every dish, I´ve had em all I have", he said laughing and patting his rather large stomach. "I blame it on the desk job but Jenny 'that´s my wife' she says it´s cos I´m a gutty old bugger, ha-ha, reckon she´s right, normally is".

"Looking at this I can see why you´ve had all the dishes" said Jill, "It all sounds so delicious, but for me it´s a no brainer, I´ll have the Sausage and

Mash. Humm! It says, 'Bridgetown farm pork sausages on spring onion mash with a delicious onion gravy' I cannot wait".

"And the same for me", said Dan.

"Ha-ha! That's three of us, the sausage and mash is my favourite too" said Bernie with a beaming smile as he went off to the bar to place their orders.

When Bernie returned to the table he tapped Jill on the arm and said "I am so sorry about your friend, Jill and pleased that you are okay. I was the one who received your mayday broadcast that night, it was a bad storm indeed. But as I said to Dan the other night it's a good thing that he spotted you, it's not easy spotting people in the sea".

"Thank you" said Jill "It was a frightening ordeal for sure. As sailor's we like to think we are ready to cope in all weathers, but mother nature was in charge that night, we were just hanging on...

Well, I'll recommend this pub to everyone from now on" said Jill, "That was absolutely delicious, I only hope the new chef on 'Solent Sam' can cook this good" she said laughing.

Dan raised his finger and said to Bernie "That'll be me she's talking about, Bernie".

"You wanna get him to do one of his paellas" said Bernie to Jill.

"He did" said Jill "That's why he's got the job" and they all had a good laugh.

They had one more drink, said their goodbyes and made their way back to the cove.

"What a lovely man Bernie is" said Jill as they walked along the coastal path.

"Yep, he's a smashing lad indeed. Do anything for anyone if they're in need", said Dan.

When they got back to the cove, Jill went aboard the Arvor and Dan to the boathouse. An early night for both as they were setting off at sparrows in the morning. Before Dan went to bed he packed a pair of slacks, a jacket, shirt and tie into his suit carrier and shoes in his bag. He then set his alarm for five thirty, climbed into bed and quickly drifted off into the land of nod.

-:T:-

Chapter Seven

Jill sat up and turned off her alarm, it was five fifteen. She was up and dressed and had the kettle on the boil in five minutes flat. At the chart table she got out the chart for the trip and checked the tides. She tuned in to the weather station and it was going to be fair all the way.

Dan was also up early and had bacon and scrambled eggs on the go and a fresh jug of coffee for the flask. He opened the door and shouted, "Breakfast is ready when you are, Jill".

"On my way" came the reply.

After breakfast Dan washed the plates and took his gear and stowed it away on the Arvor.

He locked up the boathouse and they were on their way.

"I love being on the sea when dawn is dawning" said Jill "The light reflected on the water is so beautiful".

"I couldn't agree more, especially when the sea is calm like it is today" said Dan, "C'mon let's have a drive of 'Solent Sam'.

Jill got up from the seat and said, "By all means Sir, please it's all yours".

Dan was like a little boy at the fun-fair, smiling like a Cheshire cat as he put the Arvor through its paces. "Definitely getting one of these" he said.

"Okay, now for the clue that was in the tin at 'The Kings Arms' in Weymouth. Said Jill, she put the sheet of paper on the chart table and took over the controls whilst Dan studied it.

***

'The Kings Arms'

"3, 15, 14, 7, 18, 1, 20, 21, 12, 1, 20, 9, 15, 14, 19"

Now for your clue…

The 26, 9, 25, 18, 7, 9, 26, 7, 12, 9 will ease the tensions between those affected by the 22, 24, 19, 12, 18, 13, 20 noise caused by the 9, 22, 11, 26, 5, 18, 13, 20 work party.
Between the rocks the answer lies.

***

"The first lot of numbers we checked in the book as we did before" said Jill "But it never made any sense. It turned out that the code was based on the alphabet. A was one, B was two and so on. Quite easy really. 'Congratulations' was the first part. When we tried to work out the next set of numbers it was the same story as before, it made no sense whatsoever.

Geoff realised that the highest number was twenty six so it must still be using the alphabet.

It was the alphabet, but it had been used in reverse, Z being one Y being two, and all the way down to A being twenty six.

So the clue read as follows"…

*'The **Arbitrator** will ease the tensions between those affected by the **Echoing** noise caused by the **Repaving** work party.*
Between the rocks the answer lies '.

"We typed those words into the 'what3words' app and it turned out to be the far edge of 'Fort Grosnez' on the Island of Alderney in the Channel Islands; So somewhere between the rocks in that three meter square is the clue".

Jill contacted the harbour master at Langston and was told that there were only deep water moorings available. She decided that when they enter the Solent they would call into Weymouth and collect her dinghy so that they could row ashore when they get to Langston.

Having collected the dinghy and oars they were soon on their way again. Dan was in the galley cooking a lunch of fresh Mackerel which they had caught on their journey by towing the feathered lines behind the Arvor. "I will do some savoury rice to go with the fish if that's okay with you" he said.

"That 'll be lovely" replied Jill "It certainly smells good"

"This is the furthest I've been into the Solent" said Dan "Is Langston a big place?"

"No, it's not massive like Portsmouth, or Plymouth. It's a very picturesque little spot with a couple of great pubs and a windmill that was built in the early seventeen hundreds, it's real postcard stuff, you'll love the place."

"So, this is your sailing playground, is it?" said Dan.

"It sure is" said Jill, "We sailors experience all kinds of sailing conditions here, that's what makes it perfect for us, Oh! and what a lovely phrase you used, 'Playground'. If we have enough time after Langston we can call into Cowes on the way home before heading up to York, just to say you've been there".

"One Mackerel served on a bed of savoury rice, Madam" said Dan. "I'll take over while you eat yours, mine will stay warm in the oven".

They swapped seats and Jill tucked into her lunch saying, "This is cooked perfectly Dan, you can´t beat fresh caught fish.

Not long now look, that´s Cowes off to the starboard. If you look to port you can see the Isle of Wight ferry coming out of Southampton. It´s a very busy place is the Solent".

Jill finished her lunch and took control of the Arvor while Dan had his meal. When Dan had finished eating he washed up and made coffee.

"Well, we´re making good time, there´s the Portsmouth Spinnaker Tower off to port" said Jill, "You should see it at night when it´s all lit up, it looks fantastic.

There´s Southsea Castle, we´ll head in towards Langston Harbour when we get level with Fort Cumberland. It´s high tide in about an hour so we shouldn´t have any problems getting to the mooring. When we´ve moored up we´ll row in and go recce the clue site".

"That sounds good to me" said Dan "What´s that, an old road bridge or something?".

"No that was the railway for the old 'Puffing Billy' train that used to run from Havant to Hayling Island for the holiday makers. I think it was in the early sixties, sixty two or sixty three when it closed. The wooden swing bridge was in need of repair or renewal and the cost was way too much, so they decided to close the service".

"Ah! There´s the postcard view" said Dan.

"Yes" said Jill "That´s the Langston mill on the right and just to the left of it is The Royal Oak, come round further and, there is The Ship Inn. They both do great food by the way. The mill and the house was once occupied by the writer Nevil Shute, he´s famous for writing 'A Town Called Alice' and 'On The Beach' among other books. Full of useless information, I am".

"Not at all" said Dan "I find these kind of facts quite interesting".

Having moored up Dan made coffee and they both sat relaxed for a while. Jill then continued bringing Dan up to speed on the clues.

"We had been at Weymouth for two days and on the third morning we sailed to Alderney. The weather was in our favour with a northerly wind of sixteen to eighteen knots and Wave Dancer was living up to her name".

-:T:-

Chapter Eight

'Alderney'

"We allowed for a full day's sailing and also worked out the tides for our entry to the harbour.

The tides around Alderney can be strong so it is best to err on the side of caution.

The other problem is that you have to sail through the main shipping lanes. That can be fun at times, especially if you sail at night.

We arrived in Alderney at six thirty in the evening, moored up and booked in with the harbour master before we headed to The Divers Arms for a well-earned meal and a pint, as Geoff put it.

We had a good night's sleep on the boat and the following morning we got the harbour taxi to take us ashore. We had breakfast in one of the many restaurants in Alderney and then went down to Fort Grosnez. We got to the three meter grid where the clue sent us and we searched every inch of the area but never found the other tin.

We decided to head to the Braye Hotel and Geoff booked us in for three nights. "We're in Alderney, why waste it" he said "It may be out of season but the weather isn´t too bad and, well, we need to double check this clue anyway. They have Wi-Fi here… and a rather lovely looking bar" he said, with that cheeky grin on his face.

We took the harbour taxi and went back to the yacht to collect our things and also Geoff´s laptop.

That afternoon we sat in the hotels lounge and went over the clue again just to make sure we had the right location.

"Everything works out the same" Geoff said. "Tomorrow we shall have to spend more time there" I told him "The three meter square actually goes right to the water's edge, we´ll just have to move the rocks, rock by rock, it´s there somewhere. We´ll find it, worry not".

We booked a table for that evening in the 'Brasserie' restaurant at the hotel.

We sat at a table by the window that looked out onto the white sand Braye beach, a wonderful setting indeed.

For the starter we ordered the local Crab Cakes, for main the King Prawn Scampi, and we shared a bottle of Chardonnay. After diner we had coffee and chocolate brownies, we both agreed that it was a lot better than staying on the yacht.

Considering it was out of season there were quite a few people staying at the hotel. Many of them were like us, booked in for a few nights comfort rather than staying on their yachts.

One of the guest was an old man, probable in his nineties and using a wheeled walking frame. As he made his way from the dining room to the lounge Geoff got up to move a few chairs that were blocking his way.

"Thank you young man" he said to Geoff with a radiant smile and a nod, "That´s really very kind of you".

"Not at all" said Geoff and he then asked, "Are you here on holiday".

"No, I stay here permanently, I have a suite on the top floor. The name is Jacob," he said offering his hand.

Geoff shook his hand, told him his name is Geoff and then introduced him to me.

"I´m pleased to meet you both" said the old man, "And what about you, are you on holiday".

"Not a holiday as such" said Geoff, "We are actually on a kind of treasure hunt. The clues we are following have taken us to the Lake District, Yorkshire, Weymouth and here we are in Alderney. Please, join us Sir, for a nightcap".

"That would be lovely, thank you" he said.

" Please, call me Jacob".

"What would you like to drink, Jacob?" asked Geoff.

"I'll have a 'Dalwhinnie' single malt please. If you tell the barman it's for Jacob he'll know the one I like".

"I think I'll join you" said Geoff. "And what would you like, Jill."

"White wine for me please, Geoff, I won't mix my drinks."

When Geoff returned with our drinks, Jacob said "I saw you both down at the Fort today, it looked as though you had lost something, was that one of the clues you were searching for?"

"Yes it was, but we didn't find it" I said, "We'll have another go at it tomorrow.

So Jacob, how come you're here permanently?"

"Well" he said, "I have no family now. I love Alderney, have done since I was a lad, so I decided to see out my days here. I've amassed quite a large fortune in my working life and that allows me to live here in comfort, sipping single malt in the company of nice people such as yourselves". Jacob smiled and said "Cheers" raising his glass. We all clinked glasses saying cheers.

"Here's to the 'success' of your treasure hunt" said Jacob. "And may you solve all your clues".

"Ha-ha! I'll second that one" said Geoff.

You say that you have loved Alderney since you were a lad, Jacob, were you born here?"

"No, I was born in Hampshire, we used to sail to Alderney in the summer holidays on my father's yacht. We must have walked every inch of the island in those days, my father had a very keen interest in the many forts and their history. He was always saying that one day he would write a book about them but he never did.

He and my mother were killed in a traffic accident when I was fifteen so I went to live with my mother's sister and her husband in South Africa. He was a dealer in diamonds, a very rich man indeed. When they passed I was in my late twenties and because they never had children of their own I inherited everything.

I carried on the business for fifty odd years, invested heavily and, well, became even richer.

I decided fifteen years ago to ditch the briefcase and the pin stripes as it were and spend my time somewhere where I felt at home.

I wanted a simple stress free life in a place I love. Somewhere I can sit watching the boats come and go. Somewhere where the pace is a lot slower and time is not so important. So Alderney it was, I always felt at peace here and the people are just wonderful".

"Well I have to agree with you on that" said Geoff, "It certainly acts like a magnet on me".

"We finished our drinks and said goodnight to

Jacob. Geoff escorted him to the lift and then we went for a stroll down to the harbour. The night air was cold so we didn´t stay long. We headed back to the hotel said goodnight and arranged to meet at breakfast at eight in the morning".

"More coffee" offered Dan passing the jug to Jill. "Yes please" she said "And ´ll have one of those biscuits if there´s any left".
Dan passed her the biscuit barrel and said "So, what happened next".
"Well, the next morning after breakfast we went down to Fort Grosnez and started to move rocks in the water, the tide was low so it was quite easy really. After about an hour Geoff found the tin under one of the rocks near the wall of the fort. As always a loud 'Eureka' and a massive smile as he held the tin aloft. "Ha-ha" he said, and then started his best Freddy Mercury impression, singing 'Another one bites the dust, and another one gone, and another one gone, another one bites the dust' Ha-ha" he said still laughing. "Right, shall we go back to the hotel and open it there", he asked.
"Sounds good to me" I told him.
"We made our way back to the hotel and sat in the corner of the lounge, Geoff ordered coffee and cake and we opened the tin. Inside was a

small piece of paper, I unfolded it and as I read out the note Geoff wrote it down".

***

'Alderney'

22, 5, 46.   178, 18, 36.   41, 22, 34   56, 5, 42.
79, 10, 28.   100, 18, 36.   135, 4, 32. 149, 2, 36.
180, 28, 31.

'The Voters are armed with Forks, and the Chair is owned by other gents. BRHC of D, 6R &3U, when removed reveals the final piece'

***

"The numbers turned out to be the page number, line down and the letter in that line. When we checked them in the book they read *'Excellent'*.
  We noticed that in the first sentence of the clue three of the words started with capital letters, Voters, Forks and Chair. I typed them into the

'what 3 words' app and the three meter square was next to a small building in Langston. Geoff went onto Google Earth found the area and went into Street View. It turned out to be a public convenience building next to The Ship Inn.

We had no idea what the second part of the clue meant so we decided to wait till we get to Langston and maybe then it will all make sense.

"Well, I reckon that if the building is a public convenience the 'owned by other gents' could well refer to the 'Gents' toilets" said Dan "This really is getting exciting, and the BRHC I´ve come across before, where the hell it was I can´t for the life of me think, but it will come I´m sure".

"We shall keep that in mind for when we get ashore" said Jill "I´ll make a note of it on the clue sheet.

We decided to leave Alderney the following morning and set sail for Langston. That evening we prepared Wave Dancer ready for the trip before enjoying a slap up meal in the hotels main dining room. We were excited because the clue said that we were about to reveal the final piece.

We slipped our mooring at six thirty, it was cold and the sea was quite choppy after three hours of fighting the wind the weather started to worsen. I took the helm whilst Geoff took down the head sail, bagged and stowed it and then reefed the main. The wind was now gusting at about thirty knots and creeping up by the minute. The sky was dark and even though we were in full thermals, wetsuits and waterproofs we felt freezing cold. Wave Dancer was being thrown all over the place and crashing into the waves with a thunderous bang every few seconds. We had to come off course and run with the storm.

Geoff reefed the main more to try and stabilize the yacht but the wind was still increasing. Below decks everything was being thrown about and we had to close down the hatch to prevent getting the inside of the yacht soaked.

The rain was lashing at our faces and it was near impossible to stay on our feet. The sky was absolutely black even though it was daytime and the noise was deafening. It stayed like that for hours. With the wind now behind us and only a fully reefed main sail we were being blown along at more than twelve knots at times reaching fifteen.

A large wave hit on the starboard quarter, lifted the yacht and it came down with one almighty bang, Geoff was thrown to the deck smashing his head on the main hatchway. He had a gash in his forehead and was bleeding badly. I went below to get the first aid kit and the yacht hit something, the noise was frightening and water started to gush in from the starboard side. I struggled to get on deck and when I eventually got to the helm Geoff was nowhere to be seen. The boom had broken off and was trailing alongside. Wave Dancer was rolling uncontrollably and speeding through the water. The wind was screaming, the yacht was taking in water and I knew that it was only a matter of time before she went under.

I managed to set off two mini flares and send out a mayday on the radio before it died on me.

Wave Dancer was thrown on her side and I was struck on the head, by what I don't know. Everything went dark and icy cold, and that's the last thing I remember until I was in your boathouse in front of the log burner.

It doesn't seem it looking back but we were in the storm for ten or twelve hours before the yacht went on her side and sank.

"You're lucky to be alive, it's a miracle I spotted you that night. God knows what would have become of you if I hadn't seen you" said Dan.

"Geoff said we should get into our wet suits as the weather was getting colder, so that's another factor in my surviving. It makes me shudder to think about it now".

"Tell me about Geoff, it seems he was quite a guy" said Dan.

"He was. He had a wonderful way of always seeing the good, no matter the situation. He would never give up on anything he started, he would always see it through. He was a big hearted man too, he´d never pass a homeless person without giving them something. I remember once when we were in Southampton and there was an old guy sitting on a blanket with a cup for people to put money in. Geoff had no change on him so he went to the nearest cash machine and withdrew some. He then went straight back to the old man and gave him a twenty pound note and told him to get himself a decent meal. He always made whoever was with him feel proud to be his friend. He was certainly a caring man whom I miss dearly".

"Come on then, let´s do this for Geoff" said Dan. "It´s dinghy time, I´ll row you can buy the beers when we get to the pub".

"Okay, you're on" said Jill, "Can you pass me my fleece please, it´s in the bottom right hand corner cupboard over there".

"Yes! 'EUREKA' I just knew it would come, BRHC, Bottom Right Hand Corner, you´re a star Jill. It´s the door of the Gents, bottom right hand corner of 'D'. The 'D' being for door and the 6R, 3U is bricks. Sixth to the right and third up, the clue is behind that brick. If I´m right, I´ll do the Freddy Mercury song".

"If you´re right it´s champers not beers" said Jill as she was putting on her fleece. "Come on then Einstein let´s get rowing".

-:T:-

Chapter Nine

'Langston'

Dan pulled the dinghy around to the side of the Arvor, got in and held it steady while Jill stepped in and sat herself down in the centre at the back. Dan put the oars into the rowlocks and started to row towards the shore over by the road bridge.

"You make it look so easy" said Jill. She pointed to Dan´s right saying, "Just over there by the bridge will do nicely, we´ll tie her up there".

Having got to the shore they pulled the dinghy from the water and turned it upside down placing the oars underneath. Dan tied the painter to one of the post. "It should be safe here" he said, "If it´s not" he said laughing "We have a long swim back to the Arvor".

They went up the banking and then through the white railings onto the bridge and walked along to The Ship Inn.

"This really is picturesque" said Dan "I can see why people love the place so much".

It was a sunny day and there was a chill in the air but the cold was not going to dampen their excitement of finding the final clue.

"Hang on a mo" said Dan taking out his mobile, "I've got to get a photo of this". He took a few photos and then asked Jill to take one of him leaning on the rails with the windmill and Royal Oak behind him, that done Dan took one of Jill and then they went along to the public toilet building.

"This is it" said Jill, "Bottom right hand corner of the door, one, two, three, four, five and six, three up and this is the brick if you're right".

Dan crouched down and noticed that the cement around the brick was a slightly different colour to the rest of the cement. "This is definitely the one" he said. He took out his keys and scrapped at the cement with one of them.

"This is soft and powdery, and it's coming out quite easily" he told Jill.

In less than a couple of minutes he had scrapped away enough of the cement to get his fingers onto the brick. He wiggled the brick and with hardly any effort it came out of the wall.

He reached in, found and brought out the tin wrapped in cling film.

"Present for you" he said handing it to Jill.

He replaced the brick and pressed the powdery cement back in around the brick. "That's about the best I can do, Jill", he said. "Come on, pub, you owe me a beer, we'll keep the 'Champers' for when we've completed the whole challenge".

"When shall we open it" asked Jill "Now or when we get back on board the Arvor".

"We'll do the same as you and Geoff have been doing, wait until we get back. But for now young lady, The Ship Inn beckons".

As they walked around to the pub Dan's mobile rang. "Hello" he said answering it. "Hi Bernie, what's the matter". After a long pause he said, "Yes mate, I'll let her know, everything else okay is it?". Another pause and then he said, "Will do Bernie, we're just off to the pub for a few well-earned beers, thanks for letting us know, I'll give you a bell in a couple of day's mate, bye for now". He finished the call and put the phone away.

"That was Bernie, he said that Wave Dancer has been found just east of the boathouse and his lads have recovered it to the cove ready for the insurers to examine it. They have winched it up onto the beach and secured it".

"Did he say what condition it's in" asked Jill. "No, but I don't think you'll be sailing her again", said Dan "You okay" he asked.

"Yes fine, it just feels, well, strange really. I think I'm ready for that drink now".

The bar was quite crowded but they managed to find a table in the corner. "This is nice" said Dan, "What would you like to drink".

"I´ll have what you´re having" said Jill.

"That´ll be two bottles of lager then. Will we be having a meal or do you want to get off to Yarmouth this evening?" asked Dan.

"No, we´ll sleep on board tonight and head off in the morning, we´ve got plenty of time. Bring a couple of menus back with you when you bring the drinks". Dan tugged the hair above his forehead and said, "Yesh mer Lady" mimicking the voice of 'Parker' from the TV program 'Thunderbirds Are Go'. Jill replied in a Lady Penelope voice, "Off with you Parker, and be quick about it". They both laughed as Dan made his way to the bar.

After their meal they left the Inn and went for a leisurely stroll around Langston and then down to the water's edge by the yacht club.

There were a few people packing away their boats after their day´s sailing and some were over by the club chatting.

"What a lovely setting this is" said Dan.

"If you look over to the right" said Jill, "You can see where the old railway track used to run, it´s a route for walkers and rambles now. It takes you all the way to Havant railway station".

"Did you ever go on the old train" asked Dan.

"No that was way before my time, my father did though. He used to live in Bedhampton and he´d travel to Hayling with his cousins in the summer holidays, they used to live in Leigh Park.

He told me once how he and his three cousins nearly drowned whilst swimming off the south west tip of Hayling. They were all bobbing about in the water near the shore and in just a few seconds the current whipped them all out to sea. Two men spotted them and swam out, they took the two girls in first and then came back for the boys. He said that all of his young life flashed before his eyes".

"Must have been quite scary for them, being youngsters I mean".

"Well, whenever they all met up it always got a mention, so it must have had quite an effect on them all.

"Dad said that he couldn't really swim at the time, a couple of strokes at best, and when his cousin Roy was being rescued he said everything went cold and dark as he was pulled under. That was when his life flashed. Now this is the strange bit, all of a sudden he said he was above the water watching one of the men pulling him up and then in an instance he was choking and spluttering in the arms of his rescuer. Makes you wonder about all this so called out of body stuff you read about. Anyway, enough of all this morbid talk, come on I'll row back".

"Ha-ha! Now this I will enjoy" said Dan as they got to their feet.

They walked up to the road and when it was clear they crossed over, ducked through the railings and made their way to the dinghy.

"They're an honest lot in Langston", Dan said, "It's not been nicked so we don't have to swim back".

As Jill was rowing back to the Arvor Dan said that he was well impressed and if he had known she was that good he'd have let her row over earlier.

When they got on board Dan put the kettle on to make coffee and Jill cleared off the chart table ready for them to go over the new clue.

"This is really exciting for me" said Dan, "You have been through this four times already so it's old hat for you".

"I still find it exciting though" said Jill, "You, may have the honour of opening this one, Dan".

She slid the wrapped tin across the table to Dan. He unwrapped it very slowly, trying to add to the suspense.

"Oh! Get on with it, will you" said Jill in a mockingly stern voice.

Just before opening the tin Dan blew a fanfare and then started laughing as he pulled off the lid.

Inside the tin there were a few folded up pieces of paper. Dan unfolded the sheets and placed them on the chart table so they could both see them, he then read out what it said...

***

'Langston Harbour'

*This is the **last** part of your adventure. Well done and congratulations on getting to this point.*

For this final task you will need the answers to five questions from ADIBS, and five answers to questions about the Locations where you found the clues.
This will confirm that all tasks have been completed, and that you are not just the finder of this one tin alone.

Questions from ADIBS :

1, What could be heard all over the pitch?
page 41.

2, *What was brought in on a big plate?*
    Page 55.
3, *What will also be used in court?*
    Page 71.
4, *What did Jenny give Samantha?*
    Page 178.
5, *Where was the Chapel of Rest?*
    Page 187.

Questions from the Locations :

1, *What was the name of the Hamlet?*
2, *What was Crooked?*
3, *What was next door to The Kings Arms?*
4, *What is the name of the Fort?*
5, *What is south of the bridge?*

You will find the last tin containing the name and address of the solicitors firm holding your reward at...

.--. --- . - .. -.-.   145, 10, 23.   14, 1, 23.

194, 11, 36.   15, 6, 28.   71, 4, 36.   *Mausteinen*

Remember to bring with you the answers to the questions in this letter. The book the original letter was found in, and the contents of the final tin.

***

"Okay" said Dan, "You get the book, I´ll read out the page number and the question, and you find the answer".

"Sounds good to me". said Jill taking the book out of the box along with a note book and pen for Dan to write down the answers.

"Ready when you are" said Jill.

"Page forty-one", said Dan. Using his finger as a pointer on the sheet of paper.

"Forty-one, yep! Got it", replied Jill.

"What could be heard all over the pitch? asked Dan.

Jill began reading from the top of the page. "Here we are" she said, "You could hear the 'CRACK' all over the pitch. So it was when Trevor Huntley got his leg broke playing football".

Dan wrote down the answer saying, "This bit is easy, shouldn´t take us too long at all".

The answers to the ten questions were found in less than half an hour. Jill said that the clue part was actually a lot easier than the other clues.

The morse code part spelt the word *'Poetic'* the numbers were related to the book, page number, line down and the letter in that line, spelling the word *'Porch'*. Jill Googled the word Mausteinen and it turned out to be the Finnish word for *'Spicy'*.

Dan entered the words into the 'what3words' app and the location was where a pipe runs across a creek near Bedhampton. It turns out that it was indeed called 'Bedhampton Creek'.

"Wow! Is that the time?" asked Jill, "It´s five to two. Best get our heads down, we need to be away early in the morning".

"Well, we´ve broken the back of it now, so we can leave it till we get back from York" said Dan sorting out their sleeping bags and bunks whilst Jill washed the coffee cups and checked that all was secure on deck.

-:T:-

Chapter Ten

'Off to York'

Frere Jacques rang out from Jill's mobile phone at six thirty in the morning and as always she was up and out of her sleeping bag in a flash.

Dan poked his head out of his sleeping bag and asked, "What time is it?

"Time you were up already" replied Jill in a very stern, put on voice.

"You sound just like my Mother on a school morning, five more minutes and I'll be up Mum, honest" said Dan sitting up and rubbing the sleep from his eyes.

Jill went up on deck and called out to Dan that it was overcast and looked like rain. "It'll be a bit choppy out there today but at least we'll stay dry in here".

Dan stuck his head out of the hatch, looked around and said, "It's a bit parky too, I should've stayed in bed where it's warm".

"I'll get coffee on the go" and then we'll make a move", said Jill.

"Aye, aye skipper" said Dan jokingly. Jill smiled to herself, pleased in the knowledge that Dan turned out to be a really good friend and great company to be with, after all she wouldn´t have been here if it wasn´t for him.

Dan started the engine and got 'Solant Sam' under way. They soon got to the Cumberland Fort and set a course to Yarmouth. The wind was picking up and the Arvor was getting bounced about by the waves and the incoming tide. After four uncomfortable hours they motored into the calm of Yarmouth harbour.

"Much calmer in here" said Dan as be brought the Arvor alongside the jetty nearest the slipway. Jill jumped off and secured the mooring lines as Dan positioned the buoys along the side.

"Morning Jill" shouted the harbour master.

"Morning David" Jill shouted back, "Are we okay here".

"Yes, you´ll be fine there. Not so nice out there this morning, bit lumpy I guess".

"You can say that again".

Dan came round to the aft end to join Jill.

"This is Dan. Dan, David. David Dan".

"Hi Dan, nice to meet you, any friend of Jill´s is a friend of mine", said David.

"And it´s nice to meet you too", said Dan.

"Been somewhere nice?" asked David, as he made his way down from the office to shake hands.

"We´ve been over to Langston harbour", Jill

told him.

"Lovely spot is Langston. Here, let me get that", he said taking the sailing bags from Jill and helping her down. "I heard from the coast guard that Wave Dancer was located off Prawle Point. They say that she must have hit the rocks there.

"Yes, they informed us the other day. She´s been winched onto the beach next to Dan´s boathouse. It´s in the hands of the insurers now".

Dan finished unloading all their gear onto the pontoon and Jill locked the Arvor.

"I´ll give you a hand up to the top with this lot, young Steve will run you round to the house", said David, "save you both getting soaked".

"Thanks for that" said Jill. How´s Gillian?" "She´s a lot better now thanks, you´ll have to pop round and see her. She´d love to catch up".

"It won´t be till next week now, David, we´re driving up to York tomorrow. We´re meeting up with Cynthia for the scattering of Geoff's ashes".

"Well make sure to give her our love, tell her she´s in our thoughts".

"I certainly will" said Jill, "thank you".

Steve loaded all their gear into his land Rover and they all piled in. "Right, off we go then", he said, starting the engine and moving off in the direction of High Street.

It only took a few minutes to reach Jill´s house and Dan was really impressed. It was a large white slatted house at the end of a row and had all the charm of an olde world seaside property.

At the rear of the house the large garden went down to a private jetty on the Solent. The décor inside was simple with pastel shades throughout and on the walls were framed sailing charts and nautical prints of schooners and square riggers from times long gone.

"This is absolutely beautiful" said Dan, you´ve decorated the room perfectly".

"Thank you" said Jill, "It was mostly my Dads doing if I´m completely honest but I do love it here. Put your gear down here and I´ll show you around".

After a tour of the house they went into the kitchen which looks out onto the Solent. It was a really large room and ran the full width of the property.

"This is where I spend most of my time when I´m home", said Jill, "Coffee and a sandwich for lunch if that´s okay with you, Dan".

"That will be just fine" he said. "David is a very pleasant guy, have you known him long?"

"Yes he and my father have known each other for years, he and Gillian used to sail with us on

Wave Dancer. Steve is their son and he has sailed around the world three or four times. He knows all there is to know about sailing. It's great to watch him trimming sails, whatever speed you're going at he'll trim the sails and get the boat going faster, and like David, he'll do anything for you. They really are lovely people.

After a long hot shower and shave Dan sorted out his clothes for the morning. He pressed his trousers and shirt and made sure that all was ready. Jill got their washing done and in the dryer. They spent the afternoon going through the Langston clue one more time.

"Well, it all seems to be right" said Jill, "It's really exciting knowing that it will be the last of the tins next time". She typed out the answers to the questions and printed them off, then placed them in a plastic folder with the book. "All we need now is the contents of the final tin and we're ready to go to the solicitors, wherever they might be. Oh! I've booked the ferry for nine o'clock in the morning by the way".

"Don't worry 'Skipper' I'll be up at sparrows" said Dan, throwing Jill a salute, jokingly.

Everything for the York trip was packed and ready for the morning. Jill had phoned the York Hilton and booked two single rooms for their stay, she also phoned Cynthia to let her know that they should be in York sometime around three or four o'clock in the afternoon.

That evening they walked down to 'The Bugle Coaching Inn' and enjoyed a steak meal and glass of house red.

"That´s the best house red I think I´ve ever had" said Dan, "It´s normally the bottom end plonk stuff they give you".

"We have high standards here on the Island, don´t you know". said Jill doing her best to look like Royalty looking down on the peasants.

"Ha-ha!" said Dan, "Consider I is well and truly scalded, Ma´ am". They both had a good laugh.

"Yarmouth is certainly a lovely little place", said Dan "I think I´ve been in my little cove too long. I shall have to get out and travel, see a bit more of the country. It´s easy I suppose to get stuck in ones ways. Don´t get me wrong, I really love my life but, well, it´s when I saw how lovely Langston is, I started wondering how many more beautiful places there are that I have never seen. Yep! I´m going to start getting out more".

"I agree" said Jill "But it´s always nice to get home. I travel all over and it´s great seeing other places, but as they say, 'Home is where the heart is, and my heart is here in Yarmouth".

They finished their meal and drinks, settled the bill and walked back to Jill's house to get an early night before their long drive north in the morning.

It was ten o'clock in the morning when they drove off the ferry in Lymington. They had agreed that Jill would drive for two hours and then after a break for coffee somewhere Dan would drive for the next two. As they drove they chatted about their lives and the past.

"So, how come you ended up living in your boat house?" asked Jill.

"Well, it used to belong to my uncle on my mother's side. It had been in their family for… well, certainly as long as I can remember. We used to spend our summers there, sailing, fishing and just having a great time really.

My father died when I was young so my uncle George, he was like a father to me. He taught me everything about the sea and the sailing world.

When he passed away he left it all to me along with the land and the private cove. He had no family other than my mother so I ended up with quite a sizable amount of money to go with it.

The land from the road to the cove is farmed by a local farmer so I get income from that as well".

"Have you got family living now?" asked Jill.

"No, Mum died seven years ago now, it was the

dreaded cancer took hold and wouldn´t let go.

Operations, chemo, remission, then it came back with a vengeance and finished the job. Six years from start to finish it was, lots of pain and anguish. It wasn´t an easy few years.

What about you" asked Dan.

"Similar story really, Mum passed away ten years ago, and like your mum it was cancer, colon cancer in her case. Dad went two years after her. His heart was weak, he suffered a massive stroke and died the same day.

This is us" said Jill as she pulled off and into the Northampton services. "Coffee, sandwich and cake, fill up and on our way again after an hours break. How's that sound?".

"Great timing" said Dan, "I´m ready for the loo and a coffee" he said. "We´ve made good time, the traffic´s not too heavy today".

After their break they joined the M1 and continued the journey.

"So much for me saying 'the traffic´s not heavy today', look at it now" said Dan.

"Never mind" said Jill "We shall be calling in to the Tadcaster road chippy when we get to York. Fish, chips, mushy peas, and 'scraps' remember, they´ll cheer you up I promise you".

"I´d forgotten all about that", said Dan licking his lips.

"We shall sit and eat them on the Knavesmire, right next to the racecourse". said Jill, "We can't take them to the hotel, and anyway we want to eat them hot.

Another one to remember when we head south again is the butchers in Dringhouses, he makes what must be the world's best ever pork pies. He wins trophies every year for them, he says it's his families secret ingredients".

"Ha-ha! It's all food with us, it's a wonder we're not twenty stoners" said Dan laughing.

After another two hours of driving Dan left the M1 motorway and turned onto the A64 which would take them to York. "We'll stop at Tadcaster and stretch our legs" said Jill.

"It's just down that road there that the second clue was at The Crooked Billet" said Jill pointing to the right".

"Ah! Stinging nettle country" said Dan.

"You've got a good memory" said Jill, "Poor old Geoff, he was in so much pain with them, bless him. But he really laughed when I told him that he looked nice in pink", she started laughing and said, "It's good to remember the good times".

"Yep!, always remember the good, that's what gets you through".

As they drove through Tadcaster Jill pointed

out the 'John Smiths and Samuel Smiths' brewery and told Dan that sometimes they run the brewery coaches pulled by two big white shire horses. "If you´re lucky enough to ever see them, they certainly are a sight to behold.

They attend all of the shows and summer fetes around the area.

"Keep going straight on through" said Jill. Having got through to the far side of town they pulled into the layby before re-joining the A64 and got out of the car to stretch their legs.

"Another lovely little town" said Dan, "I´ll have to tick it off my list".

"It´s not too far to York now" said Jill, "I´ll drive the last stretch. How´s your back? It looks as though you´re aching a bit".

"Just a little stiff, that´s all, I´m not used to sitting still for so long. I´ll walk it off in no time".

"I´ve just had a horrible thought" said Jill, the chip shop won´t be open when we get there. We´ll have to go out later and get some if that´s okay with you".

"That´s fine with me, Jill" said Dan, "As long as I get some now that you´ve got me drooling".

"We can call in before we go to Cynthia´s" said Jill, "or afterwards maybe, can´t let you miss out on the 'scraps', can we".

After half an hour they turned off of the A64 and took the A1036 into York.

"Now this roads takes us straight into York" said Jill "And you're in for some more of my not so useless facts".

"I'm all ears" said Dan "You carry on, I love the little snippets of information you give me".

"There's the chippy on the left, we'll be back here later. This road we're coming down is what used to be the main route into York from London. All the old horse drawn coaches used this route.

Here's the Knavesmire on your right, York race course is on the far side. Now! just there look" said Jill pointing to her right, "Is the York 'Tyburn' that's where all the public hangings took place, the most famous of all being the highwayman, Dick Turpin of cause. They carried out the hangings here as a deterrent to visitors not to break the law. The bodies would be left hanging for all to see".

"We were a gruesome lot in those day's" said Dan looking across to the site.

"You can say that again, Dan, some of the bodies were quartered after being hanged.

A bit further on we come to the Micklegate Bar, that was the main entrance to the city.

Above the arch they used to put the cut off heads of rebels and traitors, again as a deterrent.

"Nice place York" said Dan.

"Geoff always said it was History, churches and pubs". They drove through the archway and down the cobbled street to Ouse Bridge. "That pub on your right, the other side of the river is The Kings Arms, that´s the one that floods every year. If you look at the front you can see the water line where it comes up to. There´s a lovely story about someone canoeing into the bar when it was flooded and ordering a pint. I don´t know if it´s true but it would be great if it was".

They followed the road round to the right and then turned left in to Tower Street.

"Here we are" said Jill "Our home for the next few days". Jill parked in the Hotels car park and then they went and booked in. "This´ll do nicely" said Dan.

By the time they had put their things in their rooms and met up in the lounge it was four forty-five.

They walked up to High Ousegate to the 'Danish Kitchen' where they sat and had a coffee and cream eclair each.

"It´s nice just to sit and chill out after the drive up here" said Dan, "Did you phone Cynthia" he asked.

"Not yet, I'll call her when we've had our coffee" Jill said checking her watch, "There's plenty on time, it's only five o'clock".

After their coffee Jill phoned Cynthia and was given all the details and timings for the next day. They were to meet up at Cynthia's at eleven-thirty and go to Naburn from there. Cynthia had had a bad day and said it would be best for her and Dan not to come round this evening as she really wanted to have an early night. She assured Jill that she was fine and not to worry, "It's just one of my migraines" she said.

That evening Jill and Dan drove up to the Tad road chip shop for Dan's long awaited Haddock, chips, mushy peas and scraps. Dan was surprised at the amount of people cueing at the shop, and the fact that it went out into the street.

They drove down to the Knavesmire and ate their meal in the car.

"Well what d'yer reckon, tasty enough for you are they" asked Jill.

"Well, I can honestly say that these are the best fish and chips I've ever had, and the scraps are really lovely too".

When they finished their meal they headed off back to the hotel, parked up and sat in the hotel's lounge with a glass of wine each.

"This is a lovely way to end a busy day" said Dan, "How are you feeling about tomorrow?" he asked Jill.

"I´m sure it will be a very sad day, but it is what Geoff requested and hopefully all will go as planned and Cynthia will be able to say her goodbyes.

At least she won´t be alone, we shall be there to support her".

-:T:-

Chapter Eleven

'Naburn'

The following morning Dan and Jill were up early and having breakfast in the Hotels dining room. They planned to walk up to Cynthia's at eleven o'clock. Jill had ordered a wreath of spring flowers to be delivered to the Naburn Marina ready for when she and Dan arrive.

"Apparently the wreaths and flowers have to be degradable because it is on 'Inland Waterways' and Cynthia had to apply for a special permit" said Jill, "That's why there has been a delay in the scattering. It's all turned out okay in the end though".

They walked up to Cynthia's house early so that Jill could point out places of interest that they can visit whilst they're in York.

"Wow" Said Dan, as they walked through the 'Shambles' "This is like going back in time. To think this is how people lived hundreds of years ago, you can see why there are so many tourist come to York. It's beautiful".

"Wait till you see the 'Minster', it is absolutely amazing. We shall go there tomorrow and light a candle for Geoff" said Jill.

"That´s a brilliant idea" said Dan, "And a lovely way to honour his memory".

They arrived at Cynthia´s at eleven-thirty and after introductions took their seats in the hired limousine.

"When we arrive at the sailing club" said Cynthia, "We will be taken on a motor boat up stream towards York, about three-quarters of a mile.

There, we will turn around and slowly make our way back, during which time prayers will be read and music will play as we get level with the sailing club. That´s when Geoff´s ashes will be scattered.

The river bank on the club side will be lined by Geoff´s sailing friends and the club flag will be lowered to half-mast".

"That sounds just perfect Cynthia", said Jill, "And what music have you chosen to play".

"One of Geoff´s all-time favourites" said Cynthia, wait and see".

Cynthia reached across and squeezed Dan´s hand saying, "Thank you for coming Dan, and thank you for all that you did for Geoff on that night".

"Thank you for inviting me" said Dan, "I truly feel honoured to be part of the scattering".

They arrived at Naburn and were met by Steve Saunders, Geoff's friend since school days.

It is to be from Steve's boat that Geoff's ashes will be scattered.

Before boarding they went into the club house to meet Geoff's friends and to thank them for lining the river bank.

The club Captain had laid on a luncheon for after the scattering and framed photographs of Geoff (in his sailing gear and smiling) had been placed on every table.

They made their way along the river and then turned towards the sailing club. The motor boat travelled slowly and Cynthia, Jill and Dan positioned themselves at the stern, with Cynthia holding the urn containing Geoff's ashes.

As they approached the club 'Sad eyed Lady of the Lowlands' sang by Joan Baez played from the clubs stereo system and Geoff's friends lining the river bank bowed their heads as Cynthia opened the urn and let the ashes fall slowly on to the water.

When the boat was about three hundred yards past the clubhouse they turned around and made their way back.

"This was Geoff's favourite song of all time" said Cynthia, "he played it every night in his bedroom when he was young, he used to say that

Joan Beaz was born to sing this song, and I must agree with him on that".

"It was certainly a perfect song for the occasion" said Jill.

"I found it all very moving, the music was perfect. How are you, Cynthia?" asked Dan.

"I´m fine thank you, Dan, I think knowing Geoff he´d have be annoyed that he missed it".

The boat pulled up alongside the club house and two of Geoff´s friends were there to secure the lines and help Cynthia off onto the quay.

Everyone went inside and took their seats for lunch.

After lunch Geoff´s friend Steve Saunders stood up and asked for silence.

"Now then, firstly I want to thank each and every one of you for being with us today. Secondly, I would like to share with you a story or memory 'if you like' of my dearest friend Geoff.

When Geoff and I were eighteen we both got employed during the summer holidays by a firm that was responsible for the security of part of the Portsmouth dockyard.

We were fitted out with uniforms and were to carry out night patrols around the vast compound. One night Geoff was walking along one of the jetty´s and he said that he could hear a ringing sound as he took every step. Baffled by this he decided to investigate as to what was causing the sound.

It turned out to be a very large stack of steel pipes, each one being about two feet in diameter and twenty odd feet in length.

You now have to imagine the scene, it´s nearly two in the morning, it´s dark and Geoff is the security officer charged with the security of the entire compound.

Geoff told me that he was intrigued with the acoustics that the pipes produced, so Geoff being Geoff sticks his head into one of the pipes and shouts 'HELLO' which echoed about three times and sounded great. HELLO, HELLO, HELLO. this is great fun, he thought.

Now, to Geoff one 'Hello' was obviously not enough so he stuck his head back into one of the pipes and started singing 'Moon River' at the top of his voice.

After a few choruses he removes his head from said pipe and notices that there are three, six foot tall hairy and very drunken sailors stood watching him in total disbelief and amazement.

"Nice to know that we are in safe hands" said one of the three, and then they gave him a round of applause. Without batting an eye Geoff took a bow and said, "Goodnight lads, sleep tight".

As he walked away he heard the three drunken sailors each with their heads in one of the pipes singing 'Moon River'.

He said that he nearly wet himself with laughter and that it saved him from his own embarrassment. Since that night he's always wondered if singing into the pipes at the Portsmouth dockyard still goes on by drunken sailors and idiot security staff alike.

There was a lot of laughter going around the room as Steve related the incident

"Will you all now, be up standing and raise your glasses in memory of our dear friend and Cynthia's beloved son, Geoff".

As everyone stood up to toast Geoff's memory 'Moon river' played on the stereo system and a thousand tears were instantly turned to laughter.

After the luncheon Cynthia, Jill and Dan said their goodbyes and travelled back to York.

Cynthia dropped Jill and Dan off at the hotel, and they arranged to have lunch the next day at Cynthia's home before they visit the Minster.

That evening Jill and Dan went to Geoff's house to collect the water colour painting of 'Watendlath Tarn', and also the journal that they both kept during their search for the clues.

They had dinner at the 'Go Down' restaurant before heading back to the hotel for an early night.

After lunch at Cynthia's the following day they started their sightseeing trip of York. Dan was absolutely amazed at the size of the Minster's interior. They lit a candle each in remembrance of Geoff and sat at one of the pews to say a prayer to him.

"Whip, do, what?" said Dan, slightly baffled by where Cynthia said they were off to next.

"No, it's 'Whip-me-whop-ma gate' and it is the shortest street in York, about ten feet I'd say", explained Cynthia. "You must have your photo taken there, everybody does. It's at the other end of the shambles".

"Ha-ha! said Dan as they arrived there, "The sign is almost as long as the street".

"If you both come up in the summer to visit me, we can walk around the city wall's, 'That' I am sure you would enjoy", said Cynthia.

"I will certainly come and visit you in the summer" said Jill.

"And me" said Dan, "I promised myself to get out and travel more once this 'Letter in the Book' adventure is over".

"About that, How is it going?" asked Cynthia.

"Well" said Jill, "We have found the clue to the final location, it's in a place called Bedhampton Creek on the Hampshire coastline.

In the tin the letter said that we have to take with us the answers to ten questions. Five about the book and five about the other locations.

We also have to take the full contents of the last tin to the address of a firm of solicitors which is to be revealed in the last tin".

"It all sounds rather fascinating" said Cynthia, "You must keep me up to date with your findings at this, Bedhampton Creek".

"We certainly will" said Jill, "We shall be going for that last tin as soon as we get back down south".

The rest of the day was spent visiting, Clifford's Tower, The Merchant House, The Viking Centre and just strolling around York's streets. It was, they all agreed, a wonderful few days, albeit a few days of very mixed emotions.

-:T:-

Chapter Twelve

'Salvage what we can'

On the journey home Jill and Dan decided that they would go to Dan's cove and stay there for a few days. Jill was keen to see Wave Dancer and what was left of her, also she wanted to see what could be salvaged.

Dan contacted Bernie to let him know of their plans to stay at the cove.

"Don't you worry" said Bernie, "Me and my Jenny will do a spring clean for you and set up a bed space area for Jill, we'll move your stuff into the slipway end".

"You're a star Bernie" said Dan, "Don't know where I'd be without you".

"Anything you want getting in" asked Bernie.

"Eggs, milk, bread, and some bacon if you could Bernie, thanks mate".

"Leave it to me Dan, and I'll see you both soon. Fair winds and following seas my friend".

Dan and Jill shared the driving on the journey back and because they were in no rush they called into service stations every hour or so.

They arrived at the cove at three o'clock in the afternoon and were met by Bernie and his wife

Jenny.

"It´s nice to meet you at last" said Jenny giving Jill a friendly hug and a kiss on the cheek. "Bernie has told me all about how you were rescued by our Dan on the night of the storm.

You´re looking well now though, I must say".

"Yes, I´m fine now thank you" said Jill.

Jill looked across to the far side of the cove, Wave Dancer was laid on her side and tied to post that had been hammered into the sand.

"It must be sad to see her like that" said Bernie, "I´ve taken some of the yachts contents out and put them in the boathouse for you. I´ve coiled all the sheets and halyards, they´re in the boathouse too".

"Thanks Bernie" said Jill, "Dan is right, you really are a star".

They all walked over to Wave Dancer, and Jill was visible shaken when she saw the damage to the port bow. It looked as though it had been ripped apart by something resembling a JCB bucket.

"You must have hit those rocks at one hell of a speed" said Dan, "Pitch black, in a violent storm, and alone, it doesn´t bare thinking about".

"You´re lucky to still be with us" said Bernie shaking his head slowly at the sight of bow.

"Anyway" said Bernie, "My Jenny has got one

of her sausage casseroles on the go and there are beers in the fridge. The log burner is going a treat and I´ve had some coal delivered as well".

"I should go away more often" said Dan.

Inside the boathouse, Bernie and Jenny had set up the table for dinner. With the log burner roaring it was cosy and warm and Bernie had put carpet on the stone floor.

"Bloody Nora" said Dan, "Where did the carpet come from".

"Ha-ha! It all come from the coastguard station" said Bernie, "It was re-carpeted out last year and I put the old carpet away in the loft, thought it might come in handy one day.

Well, it was still in good order as you can see, seemed a shame to chuck it. There´s undelay as well yer know, so it should help keep the cold out for you".

"That´s just what I´ve been needing in here" said Dan, "Many thanks indeed, do you want something for it?

"No, gratis mate, you´re welcome to it".

"Right, take your seats good people" said Jenny, "and I´ll dish up dinner. Bernie, get the beers out of the fridge please my love",

During dinner Jill told Bernie and Jenny the whole story of 'The letter in the Book' adventure, from Geoff finding the book to Dan and her just

113

needing the final clue, nothing was left out.

Bernie and Jenny sat listening to Jill's every word with absolute amazement.

"It's a shame Geoff won't get to see the end result" said Bernie raising his glass, "To Geoff".

Everyone raised their glasses and toasted Geoff.

"He was a lovely man and a very good friend" said Jill.

"Well, you've certainly seen some beautiful places on your search" said Jenny, "And climbing England's highest mountain as well, it sounds like you've had a great time".

"We did, and I loved the Lake District, it really is beautiful there. I'll definitely go back sometime in the future" said Jill.

"Well" said Bernie, "I'm intrigued with this 'three words thing', you'll have to show me how it works. I think everyone should have it on their phones, especially if they're the outdoor types, you know, hikers and climbers and that".

"This is the painting Geoff bought" said Jill showing it to Bernie and Jenny, "The clue was just here look" she said pointing to where the stone wall and the wooden fence met.

"It looks a lovely little spot" said Jenny".

"It is" said Jill, "Even though the weather wasn't that great, the beauty of the place still shone through. When we started out that morning from the hotel it was absolutely chucking it down but the views were just breath-taking".

"So, when are you both off to Bedhampton Creek then?" asked Bernie.

"Day after tomorrow" said Dan, "Jill wants to check over Wave Dancer and see what's what".

"The insurance people inspected it the other day" said Bernie, "So it may be worth contacting them in the morning, see what they want doing with it. The guy that turned up reckons it will just be scrapped. If that is the case, I'd remove the winches, compass, cleats, pulleys, and anything else that can be re-used or sold, see what they say in the morning".

"Yes, I'll phone them first thing" said Jill.

The rest of the evening was spent sat around the fire finishing off the beers and chatting about the adventure. Bernie and Jenny left at midnight, after which Dan and Jill got their heads down, so they'd be ready for the mornings work on Wave Dancer.

The following morning Jill was up first and preparing a breakfast of scrambled egg on toast and bacon. Having showered Dan came through to the living area, "That smells good" he said, I'll put the coffee on".

"Already done" said Jill, "You sit down, it's coming up".

After breakfast Dan done the washing up whilst Jill contacted the insurance company. It was confirmed that Wave Dancer was written off and can be disposed of as Jill saw fit.

The settlement figure was a lot more than she thought it would be.

"Will you buy another yacht" asked Dan.

"I´m not really sure at the moment, maybe I will when the summer gets here. A smaller one though probable".

"C'mon then, let´s go and have a good look at Wave Dancer" said Dan, "We´ll draw up a list of things to do and salvage. She can stay at the cove for as long as it takes, so there´s no rush to get the work done".

"That´s good of you Dan, thank you".

"Not at all" he said, "We want to make sure that anything that can be saved is saved, and it can be stored in the boat house until, well, as long as you like really".

They went down to Wave Dancer and started to remove loose items from inside. Fire extinguishers, harnesses, the bagged sails, gas bottles, cooking equipment and other small items. There was a lot of stuff missing from below, and top side there was extensive damage to the bow. The keel was coming away from the body of the yacht.

The boom and spinnaker poles were missing and the mast was broken.

Most of the rigging had been ripped from the deck and some of the safety rails were broken.

They spent most of the day listing and boxing the removed items and ferrying them to the slipway end of the boathouse.

"We can remove winches and other fittings when we finish the search" said Dan as they sat outside the boathouse with a coffee looking over at the sad sight of Wave Dancer.

"No more dancing the waves for her, I´m afraid" said Dan, "Maybe a Wave Dancer II come the summer".

"Yep! I think you could be right there, Dan" Jill replied.

"I had another look at the clue site at Bedhampton Creek last night" said Dan, "I think it´s best to get there in the Arvor.

Anchor up or moor up at one of the moorings in Storehouse Lake just outside the channel entrance, and then we can kayak to the site".

Dan showed Jill his plan on Google Earth and they both agreed that it was the best way. Dan had found out that the surrounding land was all privately owned. The best and only option was from the sea. "Where we get kayaks from I have no idea" said Dan.

"That's easy" said Jill, "I'll phone Paula my friend in Southampton, she's got two. I'm sure she'll let us borrow them. I'll ring her tonight and we can call in before we head back to Yarmouth".

-:T:-

Chapter Thirteen

'Bedhampton Creek'

Having collected the two Kayaks from her friend Paula in Southampton, Jill and Dan made their way back to Yarmouth .

They spent a few days sorting out everything they needed for the trip and loaded it all into the Arvor.

"I think it might be a good idea to have a practice with the kayaks before we set off" said Dan, "They seem to be a sit on, as opposed to a sit in type thing, I´ll definitely need a few hours to get the feel of it".

"We´ll try them out from the jetty before taking them to the Arvor" said Jill.

They carried them down through the garden to the jetty. Dressed in wet suites and wearing life jackets they got in and off they went.

"This is great fun" said Dan, "And a lot easier than I thought it would be. I shall be adding one of these to my list".

They spent a couple of fun filled hours kayaking around the Yarmouth coastline before heading back to Jill´s jetty and calling it a day.

"Well" said Jill, "The hardest bit was the

getting in and out, the paddling bit was easy, and great fun as well, I must say.

They decided that they would set off for Bedhampton Creek the following morning.

They were both up early and drove down to the harbour. The two kayaks were tied to the roof of the Arvor's cabin and the paddles were stored inside. Jill had walked up to David's house to visit Gillian whilst Dan drove the Land Rover back to Jill's house and locked it away in the garage.

"You look really well, Gillian" said Jill, "It's lovely to see you again. Are you feeling as good as you look" she asked.

"I feel fantastic" answered Gillian, "They say that I'm totally clear and will make a full recovery. Although it wasn't pleasant the chemo was successful, but I'm glad that it's all over, ha-ha, and my hair is starting to grow back. My collection of head scarfs will be resigned to the drawer. And how are you my dear?" she asked, "I hear that Wave Dancer is to be no more".

"No, she is to be scrapped, well, what's left of her that is" said Jill, "She served us all well, but I've decided that there may be a Wave Dancer II come the summer".

"David says that you are off on another jolly today, you make sure you stay safe young lady".

"I will do" said Jill as she said goodbye and

told Gillian that she would see her again when she gets back.

Jill walked back to the harbour and met up with Dan on the Arvor.

"We ready then" asked Dan "Here's the garage key, she's locked away safely and all the lights are off".

"The weather report says there will be wintery showers later so we can expect a cold one" said Jill looking up at the sky.

"Well, no one ever told me life would be easy" said Dan, "Why kayak in warm water when you can do it in freezing water" he said laughing, "Mind you, looking at the clue site on Google Earth it looks as though the whole area is over grown with weeds, and what could possibly be 'nettles', in for a penny as they say".

"Okay, let's get on before you talk me out of it" said Jill laughing.

Dan started the engine and Jill let go the mooring lines and they were on their way.

"Fair winds" shouted David from the office window as they motored slowly out of the harbour.

As Dan was taking the Arvor into the Solent, Jill was entering the weather report and their destination into the log. After about twenty minutes into their journey the sea started to get a little choppy and it began raining, which soon turned into sleet.

"They were right about the 'wintery shower' bit" said Dan as he reduced speed slightly in an attempt to give them a more comfortable ride.

Jill filled the kettle and put in on to boil for coffee. "I´ll make coffee now" she said, "Before it gets a bit too lumpy".

"We must want our heads looking at" said Dan, "It´s nice though, sat in side watching the sleet (which was rapidly turning into snow) coming towards you".

"It´s best driving at night" said Jill, when the snow is coming at you, that´s a wonderful experience".

"Talking of wonderful experiences, if you look in my bag you may just find a couple of chocolate covered cream filled eclairs to go with that coffee" said Dan.

"When did you get these" asked Jill.

"While you were at Gillian´s. I also got us some pork pies to go with the sandwiches for lunch".

"You are a star" said Jill, passing a mug of coffee to Dan, "Sandwich?" she asked.

"Please" said Dan, "I´ll have the cheese and Branston".

As Jill passed the sandwich to Dan she said,

"You told me that you spent some time in the Netherlands when we were at the cove the other day going through the clues. When were you there?".

"Years ago. It was when I was eighteen. Me and a few friends went over to Nijmegen and done the 'Nijmegen Marches'. It´s twenty-five miles a day for four days. There are thousands of people that do it, people of all ages. It´s been going on for years. Got the medal somewhere. You should put it on your list, Jill.

Anyway, when it was over we decided to stay there for a few months working for a miller at an old windmill. Ruben, his name was, great guy.

He had named the windmill 'Emma' and had a big sign on it saying so. It was still in working order and there was a café, bakery, and souvenir shop attached to it, you know, postcards, little model windmills and bread, that sort of thing.

Local school kids used to visit and be shown around, and Ruben would explain to them how the grain was ground into flour. It really was a wonderful time we spent there".

"Who´d have thought that that trip would help you solve a clue in later life" said Jill.

"We´re coming up to Cowes, I´ll head over towards Portsmouth now" said Dan.

"I´ll take over for a bit" said Jill, you can relax for a while".

"Yep! I might just stretch out and have five minutes. Power naps they call em, I´ll wake up ready and raring to go again, you watch".

After an hour or so it was starting to snow quite heavily, and Jill was finding it difficult to see.

She woke Dan from his so called 'Power Nap' and said, "I hope you´re ready to go again, I could do with some help to see where we are going. It´s getting quite bad out there".

"Bloody Nora, you´re not wrong Jill, wintery showers they said, and they weren't wrong either".

Dan took over the helm and reduced the speed which actually made it a bit easier to see. The wind had dropped and the sea was not so lumpy.

"That´s better" he said, "I don´t know about you, but I reckon a cup of 'Rosey' and a cream eclair might just go down a treat".

"I think you could be right there, Dan, and when we´ve finished them off we can start singing 'We´re all going on a summer holiday'.

After a few seconds for it to register, Dan burst out laughing and then they both started to sing at the top of their voices that old Cliff Richard classic.

"Great weather for Kayaking" said Jill, when

they finally stopped singing.

"It´s getting a little bit cold in here now, I´ll put the heater on for a while" said Jill.

"We´re coming up to the Cumberland Fort" said Dan, "So it won´t be too long now before we´re at Storehouse Lake and moored up".

"I think the sensible thing to do is call The Ship Inn at Langston and book a couple of rooms for a few nights and wait for the weather to sort it´s self out. What say thee Einstein?" asked Jill.

"Yeah, it makes sense, we´d look a right pair of Charley's climbing out of a motor boat and Kayaking up to Bedhampton in this weather".

"Just as well we kept the dinghy tied to the stern" said Jill, "We´ll need it to get to the shore".

Jill contacted the Langston harbour master and paid for a mooring and then booked two rooms at The Ship Inn.

Dan was humming Cliff´s Summer Holiday as they arrived at the mooring. Jill took over the helm while he went topside and secured 'Solent Sam' to the mooring line.

Dan then untied and stored the two Kayaks below and pulled the dinghy around to the side and secured it.

They packed all they would need for a few days into their sailing bags and made their way ashore having locked the Arvor.

It was still snowing really hard and the sky had now darkened.

"Good decision of yours to come here" said Dan, "It would have been quite bleak staying onboard tonight".

"I shall be having a nice long hot bath when we´ve booked in" said Jill, "The cold is getting to me now".

The following morning it had stopped snowing and the weather was more settled, the sea though was still very choppy so they decided to leave it for another day before heading to the creek.

Whilst they were having a late brunch at the 'Ship' Dan got talking to one of the other guest having lunch. A man in his seventies, he had an air of authority about him coupled with a really friendly smile.

"I saw you two coming in yesterday" he said, "Not nice out there, had you come far" he asked.

"From Yarmouth" said Dan, "We´re heading to the creek at Bedhampton to do some Kayaking but the weather changed our minds for us".

"I used to go to Bedhampton Creek a lot when I was a lad" said the old man, "Me and my cousin Pete used to ride there on our bikes, and then go swimming. It´s all changed now though. There was no motorway there in those days, and no posh houses either. It´s all private land now. In my younger days it was all open fields, all the way to the sea.

It was a real beauty spot, what with the railway arches and the creek itself. We used to climb up onto and walk across the big black pipe, that's still there mind" he said.

"So you've lived here all your life have you" asked Jill.

"Well, not really, I was born in Pompey and when I was five we moved to Leigh Park, lived there for years we did. Later on I served a spell in the army and then joined the Police. When I retired we bought a house on Hayling Island just over the bridge, been there ever since.

Ah, here's my good lady now, Elaine, 'she who must be obeyed' ha-ha".

"I hope he hasn't been boring you" said Elaine his wife.

"Not at all" said Jill, "We've been having a lovely chat about the creek at Bedhampton. We are going there tomorrow to do some Kayaking".

"Rather you than me in this weather, said Elaine, "Cold water and I don't get on well, ever since my darling husband here capsized the fourteen foot 'Scorpion' we were sailing one day". She glanced at her husband giving him a mock look of disapproval and said, "We should have called him 'Uncle Albert'. Everyone had a good laugh about it, even the guy behind the bar.

We chatted for about five more minutes and then her husband said that they must be on their way, and leave us good folk in peace.

"Enjoy your Kayaking tomorrow" they both said as they made their way to the door.

"What a lovely couple they were" said Dan.

The following morning it was much brighter and the sea was calm. The sun was shining but it was still very cold.

Dan took the Arvor out and they headed around to Storehouse Lake where they found plenty of free moorings. They moored up and then changed into their wet suits.

Having made sure all was locked and secure they both set off towards the first of the road bridges on Harts Farm Way.

"This is great fun" said Jill, as they were coming level with the Broadmarsh Park Slipway on their left. Up ahead on the right was what looked like a sand and cement type compound.

They were both paddling steady and it did not take too long to come to the first bridge.

They went under the first bridge and continued on to the larger bridge which takes them under the motorway. Once under that bridge they entered Bedhampton Creek (which is officially called

Brockhampton Mill Lake) as he was informed by the guy they met in The Ship Inn who was doing a rather good impression of Michael Cain saying, "Not a lot of people know that".

In front of them was the black pipe which runs over Hermitage Stream.

The three meter square the clue is hidden in is where the left hand support of the pipe stands.

Jill got to the support first and tied her painter to one of the trees on the bank.

Dan pulled up alongside Jill and also tied up, saying "Well, it´s about five or six feet deep here, which isn´t too bad if we have to get in".

They started looking around the base of the support and underneath of the pipe.

"Can´t see anything" said Jill, "How about you?" she asked Dan.

"No, nothing" came the reply, "It could be on the top of the support where it meets the pipe. I´m going to have to stand up on the kayak in order to get up there. If we tie the kayaks to the support with yours on the outside you may be able to steady mine as I stand up on it. This is going to be fun" he said, "Still, no one ever told me that life was going to be easy".

Jill positioned her kayak next to Dan´s and tied it to the support.

"Ready when you are" she said, pulling a face of

uncertainty.

Dan very carefully brought his feet up, held onto the sides of his kayak and started to stand up. After a few wobbles and shakes he managed to stand up and reach the top of the support.

"Wish I'd spent some time in the gym" he said over his shoulder to Jill, "I've got to pull myself up onto the support now".

Making sure that he had a good firm grip, he took two deep breaths and pulled himself up and onto the pipe.

The top of the support was covered in grass, moss, and weeds. Dan started pulling it all away so that he could see where the pipe sits on the support. He worked his way around to the far side and when the last of the grass was removed he could see a gap between the pipe and the support.

"There's a gap here" he told Jill, as he reached in. He felt around inside the gap and there was a length of cord tied to the inside rail. He started to slowly pull the cord up giving a running commentary to Jill as he did so.

"This is like the one at The Crooked Billet" said Jill, "That too was on the end of a length of cord". "Eureka" said Dan, lowering the cord with the plastic covered tin attached down to the waiting hands of Jill.

"Looks like it's that promised 'Champers' tonight" he said, wondering how the hell he was going to get back down safely into the kayak.

As he lowered himself down from the support, Jill held onto and guided his foot to the centre of his kayak. After a lot of wobbling and near toppling Dan managed to sit in the kayak and steady himself.

"I should get a 'Blue Peter badge' for this" he said, as he released his kayak from the concrete support.

Jill tucked the tin into her wet suit and then they started their journey paddling back to the Arvor.

By the time they got back on board it was two-thirty in the afternoon. They decided that they would head straight back to Yarmouth and open the tin there.

Jill took the controls and Dan began cooking their lunch which was pre-cooked beef stew from Jills freezer. It had defrosted and went straight into a saucepan to be heated up.

He then cut the baguette into thick slices and lunch was ready in no time at all.

"You do a 'mean' beef stew, I must say" said Dan, tucking into it as though he had not eaten for days.

When he had finished his meal he took over the controls from Jill whilst she ate hers.

"It must be the cold that makes me so hungry" she said, "This should warm us up nicely".

As they entered the Solent, Dan opened the throttle and increased the speed to ten knots.

They made great time and were back in Yarmouth at five o'clock.

-:T:-

Chapter Fourteen

'The final tin'

That evening, having showered and changed into more comfortable clothes Dan and Jill sat at the kitchen table with a bottle of wine and a pizza.

The final tin was in the centre of the table still holding on to its secrets, and they had agreed to open it when they´d finished eating.

"I´ve been thinking about this adventure" said Dan, "It would have been nigh on impossible to find the clues without the internet, mobile phones, or laptops... Well! it would have been a damn sight harder, put it that way".

"It has certainly been a lot of fun though" said Jill, wiping her lips, "That was a lovely pizza, more wine?" she asked.

"Don´t mind if I do" said Dan holding out his glass for a refill.

"Here we go then, the last tin" said Jill removing the cling film.

"Please don´t be that 'April Fool' I mentioned when we first met", said Dan with his hands together as though praying.

Jill removed the lid, and inside there was a sheet of folded paper and a small package.

The package was about three inches by one and a half inches, and half an inch in thickness.

Jill placed the little package on the table and unfolded the sheet of paper.

She placed it so they could both see it, and read out what it said…

***

'Bedhampton Creek'

I congratulate you on coming this far and I sincerely hope that you have enjoyed your journey and the locations where the clues were hidden.

Each of the locations have meant a lot to me during my lifetime, and now I am sure they will mean a lot to you.

You now need to visit Hammond-Dickinson & Dean, Solicitors at 'Carlyon House' Lower Street, Pulborough W. Sussex. They are handling this matter on my behalf and holding your reward.

On your arrival all you need to do is say…
'Our search is complete and we have the Faraday Key'.

J.R.Faraday

***

"Looks like we´re on the homeward stretch" said Jill, "What´s in the package?"
Dan un-wrapped the little package and inside there was a key.

"Wonder what this opens" said Dan, "It looks like one of those safe deposit box keys, there´s a number on it, *five-six-four*".

"It could very well be" said Jill, "We´ll soon find out once we get to the solicitors. What do you think, a couple of days chilling out and then head over to the mainland and Pulborough?".

"You´re the boss" said Dan, "It´s good with me whatever we do. Don´t forget, you have to call Cynthia and update her, she´ll be wondering how we´re getting on".

"Yes" said Jill, "You´re right, I´ll call her in the

Morning, but for now, there's a tub of 'Rum n Raisin' in the freezer, fancy some?".

"Consider my arm well and truly twisted" said Dan, "I'd absolutely love some".

The following morning Dan washed down and dried the two kayaks ready to return to Paula in Southampton.

Jill contacted Cynthia and brought her up to speed on the Bedhampton trip and the solicitors in Pulborough. Cynthia thought that it was all starting to get rather exciting and wished them both the best of luck.

Jill booked the ferry for the following morning from Cowes to Southampton, making it easier to get to Paula's to return the kayaks.

The afternoon was spent filling the Land Rover Evoque and catching up with their laundry.

Jill boxed up everything that she and Geoff had collected. The clues, the tins, and the photos they took of the locations.

She also put the folder with the answers to the questions in the box along with the key.

"Just want to be sure that we have anything that they may ask us for" she said, "I'd hate to get there and not have what is required".

"Belt and Brasses" said Dan, "Best to be safe".

They drove off the ferry at ten in the morning and made their way to Paula's house at 'The

Beeches'. Paula was not in, apparently she was at B&Q buying paint and things for a week's decorating that she and her house mates had planned. Adam and Rachell helped get the kayaks off the roof rack and into the garage. From Paula's house they drove up to, and joined the motorway in the direction of Portsmouth and Chichester.

"Shouldn't take us too long" said Dan, "I notice that you never seem to use the sat-nav Jill, don't you trust it?".

"No, it's not that. I have this thing where I can look at a map and I just seem to know where I'm going. I have a wonderful sense of direction as my Dad used to say, and because I do a lot of driving all around the country I suppose".

"Have you been to Pulborough before" asked Dan.

"I've driven through it before on my way to and from Gatwick when I used to go long haul in my younger days, but not for a long time now".

After Chichester they turned off the A27 at the Fontwell race course and on to the A29 which will take them all the way to Pulborough.

"Wow! That's some view" said Dan as they got to the top of Bury hill, "It's certainly beautiful countryside, that's for sure".

The road wound its way through the villages of

Bury, Watersfield, and Coldwaltham before coming into Pulborough.

Jill turned right at the mini roundabout and straight on at the next.

After a few minutes Dan spotted Carlyon House on the right. They took the next right which led them into a car park.

They parked the car, collected the items needed from the boot and then made their way around to the solicitors office.

The brass plate on the door said Hammond-Dickinson & Dean Solicitors.

They went in and the receptionist sat at the only desk in the room looked up, smiled a lovely warm smile and asked, "How may I help you?".

"We would like to see either, Mr Hammond, Mr Dickinson or Mr Dean, please", asked Dan.

"Do you have an appointment, Sir" asked the receptionist.

"No, we don´t I´m afraid" said Dan "But could you tell him that 'Our search is complete' and that 'We have the Faraday Key, I´m sure he´ll understand".

"Please take a seat, I will see if he can see you". The receptionist went over to a door at the far end of the room, knocked twice and waited to be told to enter.

She entered the room and closed the door behind her.

"Sorry to trouble you Mr Hammond, but there`s a couple wanting to see you. They say that (she referred to the note she had made) 'Our search is complete and we have the Faraday key'.

"Oh! My word, please, show them in Janette, and ask Mr Dickinson if he would come through with the 'Faraday' box".

"Certainly, Sir" said Janette. She went out and asked Dan and Jill to come through.

"Mr Hammond will see you both now" she said holding the door for them.

Mr Hammond stood up from his desk and came around to the front to welcome and shake hands with them both.

"Please take a seat, we´ve been expecting you" he said, "Or expecting somebody with the key"

The door opened at this point and in came another man carrying what looked like a double sized box file.

"This is Mr Dickinson, one of my partners" he said.

Everyone shook hands and politely introduced themselves.

"So, it´s, Miss Jill Marshall and Mr Dan Bridge" he said writing down their names, "Is that correct".

"Yes" they both answered in unison.

"I think it may be best if I outline things first and then we can get into the nitty-gritty.

Firstly, we 'Hammond-Dickinson and Dean' Solicitors are representing Sir J.R. Faraday, and we have been instructed to carry out his wishes in this matter.

Now, do you have the items that were listed in the Langston clue".

"Yes, we do" said Jill.

Reading from the file Mr Hammond said, "One. The book that the letter was found in".

Jill took the Book from the box and handed it to Mr Hammond.

"Two. The answers to the ten questions".

Jill passed the printed answers across to him.

"And third, the contents of the last tin".

Jill gave him the letter, the tin, and the key.

"Please, if you'll give me a moment, I need to check these answers".

"Certainly" said Jill.

After a few minutes, Mr Hammond put down the papers, removed his glasses and said,

"I am very pleased to tell you both, that you are from this moment on two very wealthy people.

Each of you to the value of fifty million pounds".

Both, Jill and Dan looked shocked at what they had just been told.

"Did you say 'Fifty Million Pounds' each" said Dan.

"I did indeed" said Mr Hammond, "Now if I may, the nitty-gritty.

Our client, Sir J.R. Faraday is a very wealthy man. Two years ago he was informed that he had only two years to live.

He had no family to leave his vast fortune to, so he has bequeathed large sums to charities that are close to his heart, and all of his staff have also benefited financially.

The remainder of the money will go to whoever it is that solves the clues.

He spent three months with his chauffeur placing the clues at each of the locations, and he told us that it was one of the most enjoyable things he has done in his life. The planning of, and the working out of the clues he said was immensely rewarding.

Once he had put all this into action he moved away to a place he has loved all his life. He wanted to spend the rest of his days simple enjoying his time, with the odd glass of Dalwinnie malt whisky whilst watching the boats come and go, so he said".

"Oh! My word, Jacob" said Jill, "It´s not a guy called Jacob living in a hotel on Alderney, is it?"

"Yes, it is" said Mr Hammond. "Sir Jacob Reece Faraday CBE, a world renowned dealer in diamonds.

He told us that he met you both on Alderney and that you were lovely people".

"Yes" said Jill, "But that was not Dan, it was my friend Geoff and I".

Jill related the story of the storm and Geoff´s death. She also told them how Geoff´s body was recovered by Dan, and how he had saved her life.

"What a remarkable and very sad story" said Mr Dickinson.

"Now, if I may, in reference to the key" he said picking it up from the desk and holding it for all to see, "You have to solve one final clue for what Sir Jacob says is 'Riches beyond your wildest dreams'. This is on top of the fifty million pounds each of you already have.

We shall be transferring the money as soon as we have your bank details".

"Would you like Champagne or coffee to celebrate with?" asked Mr Hammond, "I offer both, as one of you is probable driving".

"Coffee please" they both said.

Mr Hammond pressed the intercom button and

asked Janette to bring through a tray of coffee.

"This is your last clue" said Mr Dickinson handing them a sealed envelope, "We have no idea what it says as per Sir Jacobs wishes. It is for you both to open in private.

The sad news, I´m afraid is that Sir Jacob passed away two weeks ago. He did however despatch a letter to us before he died which is to be handed to you, he passed the letter to Jill just as the door opened and Janette brought in the tray of coffee and biscuits.

She set the tray down on a mahogany coffee table stood between two red leather Chesterfield settees which were only used for the more prestigious clients of the practice.

"Please, come and have coffee" said Mr Hammond ushering them over to the settees.

"Jacob was a lovely man, and wonderful company" said Jill. "We only met him the once for a nightcap, and to think that he knew we were searching for his fortune but he never let on".

"Yes" said Mr Dickinson, "He had that cheeky way about him and he would have loved it that you had no idea as to who he actually was".

"When you get back home if you e mail all of your bank details to us the funds will be transferred instantly, unless of cause you have the details with you, in that case the funds can be transferred now".

"I have my details with me now" said Jill.

"And I do too" said Dan, trying not to sound too eager to get his hands on the money.

"Then we shall do the transfers now" said Mr Hammond.

The transfers went through without any problems. Jill and Dan thanked both Mr Hammond and Mr Dickinson, and then said their goodbyes.

When they got into the Evoque they just looked at each other in total disbelief of what had just happened.

"We´ll open the letter and the clue when we get back" said Jill.

She looked at her watch and it was two-thirty. Dan was driving back, and as he pulled out of the carpark he said to Jill that everything feels a bit weird, strange even.

"I know exactly what you mean" said Jill, "I think I will be making a substantial donation to the R.N.L.I. coastguard fund. A new lifeboat maybe, I´ll have it named 'The Jacob Faraday'.

"I think I will match you on that Jill, and name mine 'The Geoffrey Taylor' in honour of his memory.

"That is a lovely gesture" said Jill.

"D'yer know what, when we have solved this last clue, I think we should spend the rest of the year setting our own clues for someone else to find. I'll get to travel and see more beautiful places, and more importantly, we'll be giving something back".

"Well, we certainly do think alike" said Jill, "I was thinking along the same lines, and what a fantastic time we would have doing that".

They eventually got back to Yarmouth at seven-thirty that evening.

They showered, changed and then opened the letter.

✳✳✳

My dear friends,

You will, by the time you read this letter be two very rich people indeed.
I do hope that you put your new found wealth to good use.
Very well done for solving the clues and finding the tins (which came from my gardener by the way, he rolls his own cigarettes).

When I met you both at the Braye Beach Hotel I was so pleased that good people like yourselves would benefit from my passing. The day I left the book in the waiting room of York railway station, I had no idea who would find it, or if it would be thrown out with the rubbish.
Imagine my delight when I saw you both searching for clues at Fort Grosnez knowing that my efforts were not wasted.

I wish you both well in all you do in the future. At this very moment I am sat in the Brasserie restaurant at the hotel raising my Glass of Dalwinnie to your success.
Thank you for inviting me to join you both for a nightcap, you´ll never know how much it meant to me at that moment in my life.

Jacob

✳✳✳

"What a guy" said Dan, putting the letter down, "He has changed the lives of so many people".
"He has indeed, and I feel that we must now do the same" said Jill, "I wonder if his motivation to help people came from the reading of the book".
Jill picked up the envelope containing the clue to the so called 'riches beyond your wildest dreams' and told Dan she will lock it in the safe overnight and that they can read it in the morning. "But now, 'The Bugle Coaching Inn' is calling, let´s go get a nice meal and some of that house red you like so much" said Jill.
"Yesh me lady" said Parker saluting, and they both burst out laughing.

-:T:-

Chapter Fifteen

'Key 564 and leather folder'

The following morning they both sat at the kitchen table with a coffee. Jill had taken the envelope from the safe and it was now time to open it.
"You may have the honour, Dan", said Jill. "It´s time to end the suspence".
Dan openend the envelope and placed the sheet of paper on the table so they could both read it…

***

'Riches beyond your wildest dreams'

This is it my friends, the last (two part) puzzle for you to solve. I hope you have as much fun working it out as I did thinking it up.

198, 10, 1,2,3,4,5,6,7,8,9,10,&11

Find it in a South American river, maybe.

90, 17, 1	92, 10, 1	43, 2, 5
67, 22, 6	92, 14, 2	139, 13, 6
25, 3, 5	17, 17, 4	
47, 9, 2	134, 23, 3	36, 9, 1
34,12,6	11, 2, 5	126, 1, 1

Now for the First Task...

Take Key 564 to
3,1,13,16,19 . 16,9,16,5 . 22,1,7,21,5

***

"It´s all numbers " said Dan, "It looks like we are going to need the book again".

"The solicitor kept it" said Jill "We´ll have to buy another copy. I´ll Google it and see where we can get it". She typed in 'Book, A Doorway in Blake Street' and in turns out that it was published by the author through Amazon.

She went on to Amazon and ordered the book "That´s that done" she said, "It should be here next week sometime".

"Ah! said Dan, "Look, it says it here, 'Find it in a South American river' that´s got to be Amazon 'as in the river' so we´re on the right track".

"While we are waiting for the book to arrive it may be a good idea to take the Arvor down to your cove and arrange for the removal of Wave Dancer" said Jill, "Get the cove looking its best again".

"Good idea" said Dan, "I´ll get some info from Bernie while we´re there on how we go about getting a lifeboat commissioned. Two birds one stone".

"He´ll need to be sitting down when we tell him what´s happened" said Jill laughing, "Just in case he falls down".

"Yeah! I have to keep pinching myself. I do so wish I had been in Alderney with you to meet Jacob and Geoff, they both seem to have been good people".

"You and Geoff would have got on well" said Jill, "So, we´ll leave for the cove in the morning shall we?".

"I think so" said Dan, "I´ll call Bernie and let him know that we´re are coming".

As they passed the Needles the following morning Jill explained to Dan that every time she passes them it´s like a new chapter in her life is about to unfold.

"And what a chapter it´s going to be" said Dan, "I bet you never imagined that this would be the outcome".

"How could I have imagined Fifty-Million Pounds, and with 'Riches beyond my wildest dreams' still to come".

"I had another thought last night"…Dan started to say

"Don´t go blowing a fuse" interrupted Jill jokingly.

"Ha-ha! That wouldn´t be too difficult" said Dan. "No, my thought was that together we could commission a memorial to Geoff´s father and his friend to be made and placed on Everest in their honour. I´m sure that Cynthia would be pleased with the idea".

"Now that Dan, it certainly worth looking into, what a wonderful thing to do".

"Do you think you will stay in the boathouse now that you have all this money" asked Jill.

"It´s like you once said Jill, you travel around and you enjoy that immensely, but it´s always nice to get home. I shall definitely put a new roof on it though, get rid of the old tin one, and I

may even treat myself to having heating put in.
I may also re-design the inside to make it a
little more comfortable, and that I think, will do
me nicely, thank you very much. What about
you?" asked Dan,
"I think I'll do the same" said Jill, "stay where
the memories are and where the heart belongs".
It was a beautiful morning, the spring sunshine
was bright and glistening on the calm waters.
The sky was clear, and from the inside of the
cabin it really was a lovely place to be.
"I think I'll put the Mackerel line out" said
Dan, "Get us something for dinner tonight".
Jill reduced the speed slightly as Dan payed out
the line and attached it to the stern cleat.
"If you take over for a while" said Jill, "I'll put
the coffee on and make us a sandwich for
lunch".
"Will do" said Dan moving into the control seat
on the starboard side of the cabin, "Nothing I
like more than to be sat at the helm on a sunny
day. Warms the cockles so it does".
"Ha-ha! You sound like a pirate, I was waiting
for you to add, 'me hearty's'.
Jill passed Dan his sandwich and coffee and
then spread herself out on the portside seats.
"You are right, Dan" she said, "This is the life
for sure".

Jill took a CD from the cupboard and put it into the CD player "You´ll love this" she said, as the 'Fisherman's Friends' started singing 'John Kanaka'. They both joined in at the top of their voices enjoying every moment of every track.

"Tell you what Dan, one day we´ll motor down to Port Isaac and watch them perform live on the beach there. It´ll be great fun".

"I´d absolutely love to do that, what´s your favourite song they sing?" asked Dan.

"For me, it has to be, 'Widow Woman' it is so beautifully sad and melodic, what about you?".

"Little Eyes' for me, followed by John Kanaka, in fact I like all of them".

"Yeah! Me too".

Jill washed the coffee cups and plates then tugged on the line, "We´ve got something on already" she said, "Fresh Mackerel is on the menu for dinner tonight".

She got a plastic bucket from the lazarette and scooped up some sea water ready to put the fish in till they get to the cove. When she pulled it in there were six fair sized Mackerel on the line.

She gutted and cleaned the fish and then put them into the bucket. She then washed down the stern and put the line away, washed her hands and went back into the cabin.

"Well, that was productive" she said, "Six, we

caught, and they're all a fair size too. If you've got some spuds at the boathouse I'll make some fish cakes with what we don't eat tonight".

"And I thought I was the chef" said Dan, "Is there no end to your talents?"

"Ha-ha! Between you and I, I can guarantee that we will never starve, said Jill".

They arrived at the cove at five-thirty and moored up alongside the slipway.

"Bernie's been busy" said Dan looking across at Wave Dancer, "she's been stripped of everything by the looks of it".

Inside the slipway everything from winches to cables and cleats had been boxed up and stored along the wall.

"Good old Bernie, that's saved us a lot of work" said Jill.

"We'll pay him with fishcakes" said Dan laughing.

"I heard that" shouted Bernie coming down the track, "How the devil are you both" he asked.

"Get him a chair" said Jill, "This is going to be good".

They all went inside, made coffee, sat down, and Jill and Dan told Bernie the whole story.

"I really don't know what to say" said Bernie, "Obviously congratulations, after that I'm absolutely speechless".

Jill told Bernie of their wishes to commission two life boats and how they intend over the years to give something back, especially to people in need.

"By the way" said Bernie, "When you said you were coming to clear the cove I contacted a brokers yard. They will be here in the morning sometime to assess what they'll need, cranes and vehicles, that sort of thing".

" Thanks Bernie, that's great mate" said Dan, "and thanks for moving and storing everything".

"I'll do anything for a couple of fish cakes" he said laughing, and they all joined in.

"Right Bernie, you nip off and get Jenny and we will get the dinner on" said Dan, and can you bring some wine back, please mate".

"Will do, I'll be back in about two hours, is that okay?"

"Yep, that'll give us enough time" said Dan. Over dinner the talk was all about the clues, the locations and obviously the money. It felt good for Jill and Dan to share their story and chat about the future plans they have in mind.

The next morning the boss of the brokers yard arrived at the boathouse at nine-thirty and assessed the situation.

"No problem at all, Mr Bridge, should only take us about an hour to get it on the truck. We'll only need the small crane. We can position it at the top there and swing the jib over, it'll reach the hull okay".

"That great" said Dan, "What time we looking at?".

"The lads will be here just after lunch, say two o'clock, be all done and away by four".

"Brilliant" said Dan, "Thank you".

Jill made a video on her mobile of Wave Dancer being hoisted up to the top of the cove and lowered on to the truck. All of the loose parts were tied onto a pallet and also hoisted up.

"That's it then" said Jill, "She's gone now".

"As you said earlier Jill, the start of another chapter, and you do still have the memories of her dancing the waves".

"Come on then, it's cup of tea time" said Jill.

After their cup of tea they spent a couple of hours with bin bags picking up the litter and small chippings from Wave Dancer from the beach.

"It's looking more like my cove now" said Dan "Let's go and make those fish cakes you were on about"

They stayed at the cove for three more days and then left for Yarmouth. Jill had received a tracking e mail saying that the book had been delivered and taken in by her neighbour.

Sat at the kitchen table of her Yarmouth home, Jill opened the parcel and said, "You read out the numbers Dan and I´ll look up the answers".

"Ready when you are" said Dan.

"Page one-nine-eight" said Dan as Jill flicked through the pages.

"Oh, it´s right at the back" said Jill.

"Line ten" said Dan, "And then it says 1,2,3,4,5,6,7,8,9,10 and 11".

"The line is the title of another book, look".

Dan leant over and looked. "How many letters are there" he said out loud as he was counting them. "Eleven, there´s eleven letters, so it looks as though we now need this book. Yes! Look, find it in a South American river maybe".

"So, we needed 'A Doorway in Blake Street' to find out that we now need 'The Story Man' to find answers to the rest of the questions" said Jill.

"Well, it certainly looks that way" said Dan, "Maybe he was a big pal of the author and is plugging his work".

"Ha-ha! Jacob, you crafty so and so" said Jill.

She went on to Amazon found and ordered 'The Story Man'.

"It´ll be here by Friday" she said, "Let´s go over the letter again, see if there is anything else we´ve missed, or need".

"This bit here" said Dan, "It looks like it may be the alphabet again. Take the key to 3,1,13,16,19 . 16,9,16,5 . 22,1,7,21,5. Let´s go through them and see what we get".

They went through the numbers using the alphabet and came up with *'Camps, pipe* and *vague'*. "This is the 'what3words' app again" said Jill.

She typed the three words into the app on her mobile and it was Barclays Bank in East Street, Havant.

"This must be where the safe deposit box is" she said, "We can nip over and check it out tomorrow while we´re waiting for 'The Story Man' to arrive. Two birds one stone, as you say, Dan".

They arrived at Barclays Bank in Havant at eleven o'clock the following morning and asked to open safety deposit box number 564. They were escorted to a small room at the rear of the bank where a lift took them down to the lower floor. They walked along a corridor to a secure room which housed deposit boxes floor to ceiling on all walls. The manager unlocked one of the locks and Jill using her key unlocked the other. They and the box were then taken to a side room. You will not be disturbed here, please take as long as you need. Just press the button here when you have finished, and we can replace the box.

The manager closed the door as he left and they were on their own with the box.

"Here goes" said Jill removing the lid, "What do you think we'll find?" she asked.

Inside there was a leather folder and nothing else. Jill took out the folder and passed it to Dan.

"When we get home" said Jill as she pressed the button to call the manager back.

"Thank you" said Dan,

The manager explained that the box had been prepaid for a period of two years and asked if Dan and Jill will be needing it after the two year period.

"No we won't" answered Jill, "Thank you, that's us finished".

They left the bank and made their way to the Ship Inn at Langston Harbour for lunch.

They picked a table by the window and ordered a bottle of Chardonnay to go with their meal.

"Tell yer what, Jill, if that windmill ever comes on the market…"

"What about your cove ?" asked Jill interrupting him.

"Yeah! You're right, I can always visit here when I get myself an Arvor" said Dan laughing.

"The bar is much quieter today" said Jill.

"Probable because it's a week day" said Dan, "Ah! Here comes our lunch" he said as the waiter came over to their table.

As they were eating their lunch two council workmen came in and ordered two pints of bitter. They had been repairing the brickwork outside on the public convenience building and were telling the barman that the original cement was faulty. Dan looked across to Jill and smiled, "I'll get those" Dan told the barman, "You're doing a great job lads" he said to the workman.

They both raised their pint glasses and said, "Cheers, that's very kind of you, Sir".

"Not at all, you're welcome" said Dan. Jill kicked Dan under the table and said "You've got some cheek" laughing quietly and trying not to make eye contact with the workmen.

"It wasn't me that broke it, it was Jacob and his chauffeur" said Dan very quietly so as not to be heard.

They finished their lunch and started their drive back to Lymington to catch the ferry. As they pulled out of the car park they saw the screens blocking the pavement and the sign saying, 'Men at work' and they both started laughing.

Later that day, back at Jill's house they opened the leather folder, inside there was a zipped compartment, Jill unzipped it and took out an envelope and a key.

"Looks like another safe deposit box key" said Dan, "We could be at this for months".

"No, I don´t think so, it said 'Two Part' so I don´t think it will take us too long".

The key was numbered 338 and had a capital 'I' engraved on it. Jill opened the letter, it read…

***

This is the last key, there are no more. You need to take key 338 to…
20, 18, 1, 9, 12.   7, 18, 1, 2.
7, 26, 15, 12, 13.   1, 13.   9, 22, 7, 18, 13, 26.
Thank you for playing along with me, and now you have all the time you want, there is no time limit to get there. The reward is yours.

Regards Jacob

***

"What do you think Jill" asked Dan pointing to the numbers.

"Well it looks like the alphabet again, we´ll try that first".

The first two sets of numbers were the words... *'Trail' and 'Grab'.*

"Well it can´t be the what3words app because there are only two words" said Dan.

"What are the other numbers" asked Jill.

"Seven" said Dan.

"That´s 'G' said Jill "and the next".

"Twenty six" said Dan, "That´s 'Z', so this one must be the alphabet backwards like before".

They went through the second set of numbers using the alphabet in reverse and came up with… *'Talon in retina'* that looks like the what3words app, said Jill.

They tried that but it did not appear in the app.

"Well, what else can it be then?" asked Dan.

"Thinking juice is needed I think" said Jill getting up to make a fresh pot of coffee.

" Trail grab" said Dan, " grab the trail or trail with the grab, grab something on the trail" Dan looked at the other words and said, "Talon in retina, claw in the eye, you´d better make that coffee strong, I think we´re going to be here a while".

"Tell yer what we haven't tried" said Jill,

"Anagrams".

"Dan got a pencil and started writing down the letters and after two minutes said "**Gibraltar,** trail grab is Gibraltar" he said, "Well done Jill, "Now let´s have a go at talon in retina".

They both worked on it for quite a while and eventually came up with **'International'**.

"Gibraltar International, it´s got to be a bank" said Jill going for her mobile to Google it.

"Yep, it´s a bank in Gibraltar, looks like another trip is on the cards" said Jill, "All we need to do now is wait for the second book and work out the rest of the numbers".

"I think the Gibraltar trip could be made into a holiday of sorts, hire a yacht and maybe sail there, What do you think?" asked Dan.

"I think sailing through the Bay of Biscay this time of year would be nothing like a good relaxing holiday, hard work more like. Picture this though" said Jill, "A private jet, champagne, wonderful meals, and personal waiter service, that´s the way we go to Gibraltar. When we get there, spa hotel for a week, see the sights, chill out, eat sea food, and drink wine".

"I bow to your superior knowledge and common sense" said Dan, "That certainly sounds like a great plan".

"Private jet it is then", said Jill victoriously.

The book they were waiting for arrived on the Friday afternoon.

"Oh wow" said Jill, "It's written in verse. I'm going to enjoy reading this".

"Okay" said Dan "Let's work through the numbers and see what we get".

As Dan read out the numbers Jill found the pages, the lines, and then wrote down the words.

When finished the message said…

'I've come to the end of my life. It is now all for you'.

-:T:-

Chapter Sixteen

'The Cessna and Key 338'

Over the next few weeks Jill and Dan journeyed up to York and spent a few days with Cynthia. During their stay they brought her fully up to date on the letter in the book adventure. On one of the days they walked around the city walls which Dan thought was a day very well spent. The ancient walls and their banks filled with Daffodils was a photographers dream he thought.

They also spent time at the cove with Bernie and Jenny. Dan employed an architect to draw up plans to lenghten the boathouse and make it two story with two double bedrooms and a bathroom on the upper level.

The slipway was also to be lenghthened to allow for the extention of the main building.

The new roof was to incorperate solar pannels and there would also be underfloor heating.

The work would hopfully take place in the summer months, if the plans are approved of cause.

When they returned to Yarmouth Jill booked a private flight to Gibraltar and two suites in the Sunborn hotel which is a cruise ship moored perminately at the marina, and also just happens to be rated five star.

"Might as well do it in style" she said as Dan looked on impressed with her organisation skills.

She had booked the flight and hotel for two weeks time as that would allow them time to shop for clothes and anything else that would be needed for such a trip.

They took the Arvor over to Ocean Village in Southampton and got a taxi from there to the Westquay shopping centre.

They were there for a full day and both of them got everything they needed.

"If there was an Olympic shopping event you´d certainly win the gold" said Dan to Jill as the poor old taxi driver struggled to get all of the carrier bags into the taxi.

"Ocean Village, please" said Dan, "And be quick, before Jill here sees another shop".

"Ha-ha" said Jill, "You were just as bad, half of these bags are yours, at least I didn´t buy a psychedelic patterned shirt, it´s Gibraltar we´re going to, not Hawaii. You´re going to look like a right walley" said Jill mockingly.

"I´m staying out of this" said the taxi driver laughing as he got in the cab and started the engine.

"Anyway" said Dan, most of us men have got a

bright patterned shirt, aint that right".

"I aint" said the cabby.

"Ha-ha" said Jill, you´ve just earnt a nce big tip".

Having loaded everything into the Arvor they headed out onto the Solent and set a course for Yarmouth.

"That, was actually a very enjoyable day" said Dan, there are so many different shops there".

"Yeah! They have everything there, and it´s all in one place, you don´t have to go miles looking for what you want".

"Bit lumpy this evening" said Dan "The winds whipping up a few white horses".

"I´ll get some coffe on the go before it gets too bumpy" said Jill, "and we´ve got those pasties I can warm up too".

"That´ll do for me" said Dan, "I must admit I am getting a bit peckish".

That evening after dinner they sat down and went through the letters and clues once more just to make sure they had everything right.

"OH!... MY... WORD" said Dan as he saw the Cessna Citation CJ3 sat on the pan waiting for their arrival. "This is certainly the way to travel, I think I´m going to enjoy this".

"You´re not alone" said Jill smiling excitedly.

"Good morning" said the flight attendant coming over to greet them. "My name is Helen, but please call me Hel".

She led them onto the aircraft and showed them to their seats.

"Wow" said Dan "This is something else".

The seating was all in cream leather. Each seat was a reclining armchair and there were only eight of them. As they sat down with a glass of Champagne Dan said, "Well, no one ever told me that life was going to be easy".

"Ha-ha" Laughed Jill, "You´ll just have to rough it for a few hours".

"This is deffinately something I could get used to" said Dan.

During the flight they were invited onto the flight deck and were introduced to the Captain. He told them about the controls, flight time, and the speed and altitude they were flying at.

The meals were of the highest standard and they could have anything they wished for if it was on board.

Helen was delightful and certainly made their time onboard not only a pleasurable one, but one they would never forget. During their flights Hel told Jill that she was studying to become a pilot hersef. Dan jokingly said " It´s bad enough with women drivers, let alone pilots".

"He's a cheeky one" said Hel, "I'll have you know I passed my driving test first time, how many times did it take you to pass?" she asked Dan.

Very quietly Dan said "Second"

"Pardon, what was that" said Hel laughing.

"Second" Dan said, much louder than before, "Okay, I know when I'm beaten" he said holding his hands up in surrender.

"Not only did he pass his test on the second attempt" said Jill, he's only gone and brought a psychedelic patterned shirt".

The two girls both went into fits of laughter and Jill said, "What a looser",

"Here you" said Dan to Jill, "I thought you were on my side, I'm getting ganged up on here".

"Us girls have to stick together you know" said Hel. "Anyway, back to work, more champagne" she asked.

"Yes please" They both replied at the same time.

Hel also brought a selection of breads, crackers, croissants, cooked meats and caviar to the table, along with coffee, fruits and pastries.

As they departed the aircraft at Gibraltar airport Dan and Jill thanked Hell for a truly wonderful fun filled time, and Dan being Dan jokingly said "You must have had a brilliant driving instructor that's all I can say".

"I did" said Hel "Tom, his name was, and he was absoluely brilliant. Would you like his number?" she asked, with what could only be described as the most mischievious smile he had ever seen.

The taxi took them to the hotel and after signing in they were shown to their suites.

Each suite had a lounge with a sixty inch wall mounted television, settees, writing desk, and a bar. The bedroom had a double bed, dressing table, a lucsurious soft sofa, and an on-suite bath/shower/jacuzzi room. All of the rooms in the suite were decorated to the highest of standards.

There was also a very large balcony with a sun lounger, table and chairs.

Both Jill and Dan´s suites were identical and had views of the rock of Gibraltar and the ocean.

They spent the evening wandering around the hotel and were amazed by everything they saw.

"Don´t know about five" said Dan, "I think it´s more like six star, if there is such a thing".

"It´s certinly a beautifully decorated ship" Jill said, "And with the restuarants, bars, pools, and amenities, everything you need is on board. What a wonderful idea to use a cruise ship as a hotel".

The following morning after breakfast they went ashore and walk up main street to the Gibraltar International Bank.

The manager of the bank, introduced himself as Diego Fernandes Moralles.

He and Dan opened the deposit box and carried it through to a side room where Jill and Dan could have total privacy.

It was a large box, abouth three feet by two feet and a foot in depth.

Dan removed the lid and at the top was an envelope with 'Open me first' written on it.

Dan passed the letter to Jill and she opened it and laid it down for both to see.

**

Firstly may I offer you both my heartiest congratulations on completing this little treasure hunt.

As I said in my last communique, I´ve come to the end of my life, it is now all for you.

My one regret in life is that having amassed such a large fortune I never really put it to good use.

This is where you both come in.
In this box you will find the details
of bank accounts and investments
that total three point seven billion
pounds, all of which will be
transferred to your names by my
solicitors in Pulborough, whom I
believe you have already met.
You will also find the name of a firm
of accountants that I assure you,
you can trust implicitly. They can
guide you (with my solicitors)
through the obstacles that this
wealth will throw your way.

I would like you both to keep the
point seventh of a billion and add it
to the fifty million you each already
have.

The remaining three billion is the
money I would like you to use to do
good for people in need, and also to
help any other worthy causes you
would like to help.

I think it may be best for you both to take some time to think about how you intend to go about this.

Enjoy your new lives, and hopefully you will experience the pleasure of helping others less fortunate than yourselves.

Yours sincerely

Jacob Faraday

***

Both Jill and Dan remained silent for a while, and then Jill said, "This in a big responsibility Dan, how do you feel about it?".

"Well, I believe, we have been given a wonderful opportunity to do good and also to live our own lives without worry or regret. I also feel that I would like to honour Jacob´s wishes".

"You have just summed up exactly how I feel" said Jill, "It does however feel a little strange that our search for the clues is now over".

"What do you think Geoff would say or do?" asked Dan,

"Dýer know what" said Jill, "He´d be like a dog with two bones. He´d be excitedly planning how we go about it, there´d be no stopping him".

"Then that young lady, is how we shall be" said Dan, "It´s like you say every time you pass the 'Needles' a new chapter is about to begin. You once said how Geoff couldn´t pass a homeless person without giving them something. Let´s think about building shelters for the homeless in his name, and after our holiday we can spend some time setting up our own set of clues for someone to find.

In the safe deposit box there were a few files containing the details of five bank accounts held in banks around the world.

There were investment bonds, bearer bonds and shares in a multitude of companies.

There were also four black velvet pouches each containing fifty large diamonds.

At the bottom of the box there were banded bundles of bank notes. American Dollars, Euros, and English pounds. They called the manager back to replace the box and with the cash (which amounted the three hundred thousand pounds) they opened their first joint bank account.

They left the bank and decided to take one of the guided tour mini buses to the top of the 'Rock'.

The tour included a visit to the caves, the tunnels, and of cause the Rock´s famous Barbary Apes.

Every two minutes Dan was taking photos and sending them back to Bernie. He´d not really been on a holiday for, well, since he can remember so he was really enjoying every moment.

At top of the rock Dan got Jill to take a photo of him leaning on the railings surrounded by apes. The backdrop being the blue waters of the Mediterranean.

"The views are absolutely stunning" said Jill. Dan received a text back from Bernie asking him where the hell he got that garish shirt from and was the ape on his left one of his relatives.

Both Jill and Dan burst out laughing when Dan showed her the text.

"Ha-ha! See, I told you that you´d look a right wally" said Jill.

After the tour they were dropped off at the top of main street and slowly made their way down to the square checking out the copious amount of tourist shops.

"Look" said Dan pointing to a bottle of Brandy in one of the shop windows, "It´s called 'Captains Blood' like the song the Fisherman's Friends sing. The tour guide had related earlier the story of Nelson´s body being put into a barrel of French Brandy to preserve it whilst it was being returned to England.

"Another bit of useless information" said Jill, "This was where John Lennon married Yoko Ono, Oh! and also where Dan Bridge wore the most ridiculous shirt ever".

"Watch it " said Dan laughing, "I love this shirt".

When they got to the square they found a table in one of the restaurants and ordered a local dish of 'Rosto' and a bottle of Rioja.

"It´s been an interesting day" said Dan.

"You're not wrong there" said Jill, "You're not wrong there".

-:T:-

Chapter Seventeen

'The phone call'

On the third day of their holiday Jill received a phone call from Cynthia's solicitors informing her that Cynthia had died.

She had suffered a massive heart attack and died in the ambulance on her way to the hospital.

Jill was absolutely devastated on hearing the news.

Dan organise a flight back to England for them both. He also contacted the Yarmouth harbour master 'David' and his wife Gillian to tell them the sad news.

The flight back to England was very much different than the flight out to Gibraltar.

Jill hardly spoke a word on the journey home, it was obvious the news had hit her hard, she and Cynthia were really close.

After they had been back in Yarmouth for a week, Dan drove Jill up to York to meet with Cynthia's solicitors.

Cynthia had planned her own funeral and made arrangements for her entire estate to be left to Jill. This she had done apparently just after Geoff's death.

"He takes with one hand and gives with the other" said Jill as they walked back to the hotel,

"I´d rather have what he´s taken, than what it is he´s giving" she said in a breaking voice.

They decided to stay in York until the funeral. Cynthia had arranged for a very simple service which was to be held at the same crematorium that they used for Geoff´s funeral.

She did not want hymns sang nor did she want a long service. She asked that it be private with only Jill and Dan in attendance. She did however ask for the 'Ballade pour Adeline' by Richard Clayderman to be played throughout the short ceremony.

The morning after the funeral they drove back down south. Jill had arranged with Cynthia´s solicitors for both Geoff´s and Cynthia´s houses to be cleared and the contents sent to auction. The two properties were to be put on the market and sold.

Jill was not up to going through this process herself and thought that it would be best placed in the hands of others.

They had been back in Yarmouth for just over a week.

Jill had made arrangements with the solicitors in Pulborough and the accountants (Parker-Peters and Brown) whom Jacob recommended to meet and discuss employing them on a permanent basis.

They also wanted to discuss the setting up of a company which Jill and Dan had decided to name 'Wave Dancer Holdings'.

The entire funds left by Jacob had already been transferred to a joint account set up by Jill and Dan that week. The three billion pounds was to be transferred to the Wave Dancer Holdings account as and when it was set up.

The investments and shares Jacob had made throughout his life were to remain in place in order to provide a steady annual income to Wave Dancer Holdings.

The joint account in Gibraltar International was closed and the money transferred to the new account.

The plan was for Jill and Dan to go about the business of who they would help, and for the accountants and solicitors to look after the taxation and legal sides.

All the required paperwork was to be drawn up and ready for signatures in a months' time when they agreed to meet again.

Jill and Dan thought that it would be a good idea to employ a PA to work with them both, and also to deal with the day to day running of things.

Having put into place the required staff to look after the smooth running of their Wave Dancer Holdings, it allowed for Jill and Dan to live their lives un-changed, which is exactly how they had planned it. They wanted the freedom to travel and enjoy whatever it was they were doing, safe in the knowledge that the business side of things was being taken care of.

In the year that followed, the two life boats they had commissioned were launched and delivered to the stations where they will operate.

The 'Geoffrey Taylor' and the 'Jacob Faraday', were both stationed on the south coast and came under the control of Bernie.

They also made a donation of five hundred thousand pounds to the RNLI widows fund.

The plans for Dans boathouse were approved, and the building work was completed by the following spring.

The builders had done a fantastic job and Dan was more than pleased with the result. The entire length of the roof was covered with solar panels and the windows and doors were replaced with modern double glazed units.

The two double bedrooms on the upper level along with the bathroom were like something from a style magazine. The entire property was centrally heated and the lower open plan kitchen and living area had underfloor heating.

The slipway end was much longer, and Dan's new Arvor could be comfortable housed within.

Jill had read of a little girl requiring a lifesaving operation that was only possible in America.

The child's parents were contacted and the operation, and travel expenses were covered by Wave Dancer Holdings.

This was one of the first acts of 'Helping' Jill and Dan had carried out.

Local hospices and charities were also helped with donations.

They also made a one million pound donation to the Battersea dogs home which was the one charity that Cynthia paid into monthly.

Jill and Dan had spent three months travelling around the country hiding clues for their own treasure hunt using the book 'The Story Man'.

The locations included Cornwall, Scotland, The Lake district, The Isle of Wight, The Isle of Man, and in honour of Jacob, Alderney.

The book itself with the letter between its pages was left in the waiting room of a Scottish railway station.

Both Jill, and Dan really enjoyed the planning and the travelling involved in the project, and could see why Jacob also enjoyed it so much.

If and when someone completes the search they will certainly do a second one, they both agreed.

During the summer, Dan took Jill, Bernie, and Jenny in his Arvor 'Solent Dan' down the coast and up to Port Isaac where they sat in the crowd enjoying the Fisherman's Friends perform their sea shanty repertoire. It was a wonderful weekend, and they all agreed that they would do it again one day.

Jill did not buy another yacht, she said that she enjoyed the 'easy' life the Arvor gave her. She still keeps its key though, on the key ring Dan made for her from Wave Dancers wreckage.

One project that Jill and Dan take a lot of pride in, is the building of shelters for the homeless in Southampton, Portsmouth, and Plymouth.

They also have plans to build and open one in the coming months to cater for the thousands of ex-military personnel living rough on the streets.

Money was still pouring in from the many investments that Jacob had made and the list of people they were helping was growing fast.

"I think Jacob would be pleased with what we are achieving" said Jill passing the binoculars to Dan.

"I'm sure you're right" he said, looking down the valley from the stone cairn at the top of

Scarfel Pike, "This is another one to cross off of my list".

"Sandwich?" she asked, offering Dan one from the Tupperware box prepared by the chef at the Hazel Bank Country House Hotel in Rosthaite, where they are staying.

"I'll have the cheese and Branston if I may" said Dan, "I've been thinking, Jill"

"I've told you about that before" she said laughing, "You'll do yourself a mischief if you're not careful".

"Hey, you, behave" said Dan smiling, "Now, what I think we should do is call into the mountain rescue offices in Ambleside while we're here and make a donation, what say you, ma'am?".

"I totally agree" said Jill, "It's another good charitable organisation run by volunteers, and they need all the help they can get. Coffee?" she asked.

"Don't mind if I do" said Dan…. "Tell yer what though Jill, it's been an interesting year".

"You're not wrong there" said Jill, "You're not wrong there".

-:T:-

Chapter Eighteen

'Rob and Amanda'

It was a cold, wet, and blustery January evening as Rob and his fiancé Amanda entered the warm and cosy waiting room at Fort William's railway station.

They had come to the end of their winter hiking break in the Scottish highlands and were catching the nineteen-fifty sleeper train south to London Euston.

They removed their backpacks and placed them on the floor and took a seat.

"Same again next year" said Rob rubbing his hands to get warm.

"Certainly" said Amanda "But next time we´ll get ourselves a decent tent, one that actually keeps the wind and rain out".

"Well, we´ve got a whole year to get all the proper gear, and next time we´ll plan it a lot better than we did this time, having said that, I thought it was a brilliant week. What do you think?" he asked Amanda.

"I enjoyed every moment of it. If I didn´t have to work I would spend my every day doing just this.

I´ll take this with me" said Amanda picking up a book from one of the seats on the other side of the room "Someone must have finished with it. It´s called 'The Story Man', it´ll be something to read on the journey home".

She put the book into her jacket pocket as their train pulled into the station.

They collected their backpacks and went out to board the train.

Inside the sleeper cabin there were two bunk beds, a wash basin unit, and coffee making facilities.

Once inside their cabin they washed up and changed into clean clothes and then made their way to the restaurant carriage for dinner.

"It was a great idea of yours to book the sleeper train" said Amanda, "This way we can get a good night's sleep and arrive in London fresh and ready to face the journey home".

"Well, to be perfectly honest, I didn´t fancy sitting up for nine hours and then have to change trains a couple of times".

When the waiter came they ordered a typical Scottish meal of Haggis, neeps and tatties, and a pot of tea to wash it down with.

"This is one of the best meals I ever had" said Rob, "Not only do I love the taste, it´s filling and it´s cheap, I could eat this every day".

"You´d soon get fed up with it if you had it every day" said Amanda, besides it´ll be a nice treat to look forward to when we come up to Scotland every year on our jollies".

After dinner they made their way back to their cabin to settle down for the night.

Rob took the top bunk and Amanda the bottom.

"I´ll have a read of this book I found before I go to sleep" she said, "Oh! that´s different, it´s written in verse, I shall enjoy this".

Amanda began reading the book, and after a few minutes she found herself totally immersed and enjoying the stories that 'The Story Man' tells in the book.

"Well! Is it any good?" asked Rob hanging over the edge of his bunk and looking down at her.

"Yes" said Amanda, "I´m really enjoy…." As she spoke a folded piece of paper fell from between the pages.

"Something has fallen out" she said, reaching to pick it up from the floor.

She unfolded the paper. "It´s a letter" she said, "Some kind of…, here, look at this Rob", she said sitting up on her bunk. "It says something about clues and a reward of a million pounds".

Rob got out of bed and sat on the lower bunk with Amanda and they both studied the letter…

***

To the finder of this letter.

The following are clues that when solved will lead you to a reward of one million pounds.
You have two years to solve the clues.
After the two year period the clues will become invalid and the reward removed from its location.
There are five clues and each clue will lead to the next, please note :

'This is Not a Hoax'

The two year period will start January 1ˢᵗ , 2013 at 1200hrs.
Good Luck, and may your journey be successful.

(TSM 9798665534251 90000)

Seventeen, one, one.
Eighty one, two, nine.
Ninety eight, eighteen, two.

Clue one:-

The executive shouts, and angers the second officer
who´s stood where the corner reaches the sea…

***

"What do you think, is it real or what?" asked Amanda.

"Blowed if I know" said Rob, "It says it´s not a hoax, but I´ve always thought that if it´s too good to be true, then it´s too good to be true.

I mean, who in their right mind is going to give away a million pounds to someone that solves a few clues. It doesn´t make any sense".

"Maybe not" said Amanda, "But what if it is genuine. I think we should at least give it some serious thought".

"We´ll sleep on it, and have a look at it in the morning when we´re fresh and fully awake" said Rob climbing back up into his bunk, "Just use it as a book mark for now, like the last person obviously did".

"What if the last person was the one setting the clues..........?"

Amanda switched off the light, and started to imagine what their lives would be like… if they solve the clues and find the one million pounds.

-:T:-

The End

About the Author

Tom Balch

The author, Tom Balch was born in Portsmouth. He served a full career of twenty-five years in the British Army. Tom comes from a military family. His Grandfathers both served in the Army in world war one, and his Father served in world war two. Tom joined the Junior Leaders Regt, Royal Army Service Corps at the age of sixteen in April 1964. He then went on to join 14 Air Despatch Regiment when the Royal Corps of

Transport was formed. During his career he served throughout Europe and the Middle East. In nineteen seventy five he took part in the 'Financial Times' Round The World Clipper Race in Chey Blyth´s yacht 'Great Britain II beating the one hundred year old record from London to Sydney, held then by the Tea Clipper 'Patriarch'. Tom has been writing poetry and verse for many years on many different subjects and this book 'Wave Dancer' is his second novel. He is now retired and living in a small village in Andalucia where he continues to write. He is currently working on his next novel…

Also Published by Tom Balch

A Doorway in Blake Street

In this heart-warming story Jim Fraser, whilst walking home one night comes across and befriends a homeless old man. The old man has had a really rough life having lost his family in a house fire. The story tells of their developing friendship and how Jim and his family try to help him get by. The hardships the old man has endured throughout his forty plus years living rough will tear at the heart.

The Story Man

This book follows the life of 'The Story Man' and his friends. It is told in verse and takes place in the beautiful harbour village in which they live.

"Day after day he sits alone
down by the harbour wall,
repairing nets and splicing ropes
from springtime through to fall.
His sun-baked face and haunted stare
tell of an arduous life at sea,
but to the locals he's their story man
telling all his tales for free".

A Million Miles

In this beautifully presented book you will find poetry and verse covering many different subjects, The author covers all of the emotions that life throws at us. Humour, Happiness, Sadness, War, Serious, Flippant, Death, Loss, Nostalgia, the list goes on and on. So pour yourself a glass of wine, a glass of beer or a nice cup of tea 'Best not all three'. Find a nice tranquil spot, relax, sip, read, and enjoy.

Words of War

In this book you will find a collection of War and Military Life poems that have been written over a period of twenty plus years. Some are included in 'A Million Miles'.

The First Three Books

My first three books in one volume. Book one, The Story Man. Book Two, A Doorway in Blake Street. Book Three, A Million Miles.

-:T:-

Acknowledgements

Roy Haines
for his help in local knowledge matters... and for
the 'Moon River' story, Yes! It was him.

Elaine Haines
for chauffeuring Roy to the creek at
Bedhampton to take photographs of the area,
even though he capsized the 'Scorpion' in which
they were sailing all those many moons ago...
Yes! It was him….. Again!

Paula (Jill´s friend)
For letting them use her kayaks.

Rachel and Adam
For helping to unload the kayaks.

Hel/Helen
for the high and justifiable praise of her driving
instructor, and for being the world´s best flight
attendant.

Janette
for the coffee and biscuits at Carlyon House.

'The Clue Locations'

Watendlath Tarn

'The Lake District'

'Where S meets W'

The Crooked Billet

'Near Saxton, N.Yorkshire'

'Span the gap & Stinging nettles'

(The little bridge is just off to the right)

The Kings Arms

'Weymouth'

'A fathom deep, by the limbs of Royalty'

Fort Grosnez

'Alderney'

'Between the rocks the answer lies'

Langston

'Langston Harbour'

'BRHC of D, 6R&3U'

'When removed reveals the final piece'

Bedhampton

'Kayaks to the black pipe'

'We have the Faraday key'

'After a few wobbles'

Havant

'Key 564'

'A leather folder and 338'

Gibraltar

'Key 338

'It's been an interesting day'

"You're not wrong there"

'If you ever find a discarded book
in a railway station´s waiting room…
check between the pages,
you never know'

-:T:-

Printed in Great Britain
by Amazon

61624125R00123